A Lab's Ears Are Made of *SILK*

A Novella

Michael-Patrick Harrington

SILK
RAVEN
PRESS

Published by Silk Raven Press
a division of Mondauk Enterprises Inc.
PO Box 31, Ambler, PA 19002

(SRP-008)

ISBN: 978-1-7365297-2-0

A somewhat different version of *A Lab's Ears Are Made of* SILK was included in Michael-Patrick Harrington's novel *Saving Magdalene*, where it was written by the main character Magdalene Harper Barrows during the harrowing events that took place in Mondauk County in the spring and summer of 2002 and 2003. It was originally illustrated by her friend Jerry Eves.

The author humbly presents the work reimagined and hopes he has been true to Magdalene's intentions and craft.

Chapters

Dedicated to
Helium Raven Teardrop
&
Sir Duke

and

Woofer T. Washington
Ernie Hemingway
Lucky
Emma Lou
Murphee
Kirby
Harper
Biscuit
Loodle-Loo
Eclipse
Pasha
Penny Buttercup
Mildred
Shouf
Cocoa
Molly
Pearl
Spencer
Magnus
Earl
Daisy
Rufus
Sandy
Buzz
Murphy
Utley
and Brookline Labrador Retriever Rescue

"The cat will mew, and dog will have his day."
William Shakespeare

A Lab's Ears Are Made of SILK

A Novella

Episode I

What Happened

Finn's mother was a Goner.

Finn wasn't sure how he knew his mother was a Goner, but he was sure of this much: she was gone. He remembered climbing on top of her and how warm she was and how he had to wrestle his brothers and sisters for some of her milk. They lived on a farm, or at least Finn thought it was a farm: lots of straw, lots of puppies. What Finn remembered best was sleeping against his mother's belly and how it went up and down, up and down as she slept too and how safe sleeping against her belly made him feel.

Then she was gone.

Or, rather, he was.

Finn didn't remember much about his First House, where he'd lived after being taken from the farm and from his mother, but sometimes little glimpses came to him and he'd become confused. Why would he have had a First House? Why wasn't he there now? Had he done something wrong? Had he been a Bad Dog?

Whenever Finn got confused, he would go and find the Boy. If the Boy was too busy for him, Finn would lie down as close as he could to the Boy, close enough to smell his feet. And then Finn's Little White Tie would slow down, and his eyes would grow heavy, and he'd fall into his ninth nap of the day.

And what did Finn look like?

Finn was black like a raven's wing except for a little white spot at the top center of his barrel chest—Little White Tie!—that the dog believed marked where his heart was. In fact, Finn thought Little White Tie *was* his heart (at least that was what the Boy had told him many, many times), and most days, Little White Tie pounded out a jubilant beat, but Finn knew the rhythm wasn't always thus, and he was afraid of the beats that had come before.

But life with the Big Uns helped muffle any ominous tempos. The Boy loved to tickle Finn's Little White Tie, and Finn loved to be tickled; it was one of his favorite spots—there and right above his tail where Finn couldn't reach. The Boy would rub his knuckles on Finn's tailbone—and *oooh, doggie,* did that feel good! The Big Uns were always saying Finn had a good heart and that he wore his heart on his sleeve. Finn didn't know if the sleeve part was true (Little White Tie was on his chest, after all), but when the Boy was away at a Sleepover, it was Little White Tie that ached like a flower someone had trod upon. If nothing else, Finn was glad his heart was marked by Little White Tie, so that he could never forget he had one—a heart that is. It seemed like such an easy thing to forget. Though, to be honest, he wasn't sure what a heart's purpose was, but it seemed pretty important.

The Boy and the Big Uns called him Finn, but he didn't know if that was his *real* name. Sometimes they called him Huckleberry, which was a mouthful, but he didn't know if Huckleberry was his real name either. The Boy said Finn was named after a Literary Lion, and though Finn did nothing to disavow the Boy of this noble notion, Finn was certain he was a black Labrador retriever.

In the First House, he thought he had a different name, but he couldn't remember what it was. The First House was a house of Yellers. He sort of remembered hearing some names that didn't sound so nice shouted to him from the other side of closed doors. These thoughts and remembered shouts made his thick body tremble, and whenever they came, Finn would seek out the Boy.

In the end, he was Finn and that was good enough for him. Old Finn, they called him once in a while, although he didn't feel old. Sixty-three in human years, they said, but Finn wasn't very good at math, and that embarrassed him, so he would just wag his tail and accept the Big Uns' ear tickles and belly rubs.

But just lately, Finn had noticed a few changes in himself. He slept more, for one. Finn enjoyed sleeping. He liked dreaming too— just not of squirrels. See, Finn loved to chase squirrels when he was awake. But a squirrel had doubled back on him once by the old mimosa stump, and Finn ran away, his tail tickling his undersides. Imagine! A squirrel chasing a Labrador retriever! Finn had nightmares of squirrels—and of that squirrel in particular—but mostly he dreamed of the Boy and of cookies. Finn loved dog cookies; he was a cookie connoisseur. Sleeping more meant more dreams about cookies, and dreaming about cookies made him look forward to eating some.

Sleeping more wasn't the only change he'd noticed. Finn found his legs were slower, his joints achy, and his vision wonky. These were most noticeable when he and the Boy played basketball. The orange-and-blue-striped basketball (it wasn't regulation size) had come with Finn to the Second House—the Big Uns' house. Finn could just about hold the ball between his jaws, but you should have seen him dunk it in the laundry basket! During a game, the ball would eventually become covered in drool, and Finn would have trouble picking it up. Then the Boy would rub his ears and feed him a cookie, and Finn would fall asleep with his big noggin in the Boy's lap. If this was getting older, Finn thought, it wasn't so bad.

Basketball was Finn's favorite activity. The game was not without its issues however. He couldn't dribble because dogs can't dribble. Finn couldn't pass either, but not because Labrador retrievers don't like to share—Labs are a friendly sort, by and large—but simply because he was a dog. The lack of an opposable thumb was at the center of many of his sports-related issues, but Finn worried not a lick about them. If the Boy or one of the Big Uns threw the ball, Finn would retrieve it. Almost any ball would do, but the little basketball— well, that required a *unique* skill. See, it's rare that Labrador retrievers (or any dogs, to be up front about it) are involved in basketball. Finn was unaware of this distinction (among others) that separated him from his breed (and other dogs); Finn just loved the basketball. He thought of it as an extension of himself—literally—just orange and blue and round rather than furry and black and round (and long).

Every night, Finn followed the Boy up to his room and watched the Big Uns tuck him in and read him stories from the Blue Books— the ones about two brothers, both hardy—and occasionally from the Yellow ones that the older girl cousin had given him; those weren't about the brothers but rather about a girl sleuth called Nancy. (Favorites among the Blue Books were *The Shore Road Mystery* and *The Missing Chums*.) Sometimes the Big Uns and the Boy would clasp their hands together and stare at the ceiling before turning off the Boy's light. Finn stayed very quiet during these times, but as soon as the Big Uns left, Finn clambered into the Boy's bed and licked his face once or twice before snuggling up next to him. The Boy was warm when Finn was cold. He let Finn sleep on top of the cool sheets when Finn was hot.

And every single night—except those terrible, terrible times when the Boy went to Sleepovers and Finn had to stay in the Boy's room by himself (it was so scary those nights that Finn would sneak down the hall to see if the Big Uns would let him in their bed, but even if Finn managed to climb in, one of the Big Uns would eventually ask him to leave)—every single night, the Boy brought his soft Boy hands to Finn's noggin and would slowly run his fingers down Finn's very soft ear flaps. And every night the Boy would whisper the same words into Finn's ears:

"A Lab's ears are made of silk."

Finn took this to be a Truth, up there with "Basketball is Fun" or "Cookies are Good Eating."

"A Lab's ears are made of silk," the Boy would whisper.

Finn didn't know what silk was exactly, but it sure sounded like something special.

Silk.

Actually, Finn imagined the word in capital letters: *SILK.*

SILK was precious.

SILK was important.

SILK was a necessity.

Finn didn't actually think of those big words—precious, important, necessity—as much as he felt them deep inside his chest, and the words would fill him up, and he would sleep the best sleep there was, and Finn would dream of the Boy.

He was just an average boy: dirty-blonde hair, little round face, a laugh like he had a belly full of cookies. The Boy liked to laugh. Finn believed the Boy liked throwing the little basketball more than Finn liked retrieving it! The Boy sang into his hairbrush (and Finn's tail) and splashed Finn from the bathtub and stared really, really hard at books Finn couldn't make heads or tails of. Once in a while, the Boy would read to him, and although Finn didn't understand most of it, he liked to hear the Boy master the big words and swagger his way through the little ones. Finn would lie next to the Boy, and when the story was finished, the Boy would remind Finn that his ears were made of *SILK.* It was a struggle, but Finn tried to stay awake at night until the Boy was asleep. Finn considered it part of his job, and he was happy to do it.

Now the Boy wasn't much of a boy anymore, if you know what I mean. He had grown into someone you would like too—like someone you will grow into. Finn was beyond fond of the Boy— Finn loved him so much that the days when the Boy came home later than usual (or when he went to the *d*readed Sleepovers), Finn's chest hurt so bad he thought it would burst and all the cookies he had ever eaten would be revealed to all the Wold.

(It should be noted that while dogs have excellent hearing, they sometimes hear words wrong, so "world" becomes "Wold" and "bless you" becomes "blesh you," for instance. The words tend to change from breed to breed, and the phenomenon occurs even after exposure to a beast of a book so large it has two names, Merriam and Webster. Other animals in the same area of the Wold are similarly affected.)

As for the Big Uns: they were nice people too. Mommy Big Un was pretty and always smelled like you'd think a tickle would smell like. She didn't pet Finn very often, but she always made sure he had his cereal and his water, and she took the Boy to buy Finn a new toy now and again. Sure, she'd yell at Finn to stop chasing Alley Cat whenever his archnemesis crept into the backyard, but Finn got the idea that Mommy Big Un didn't really like cats all that much, and that all the yelling was to scare Alley Cat, who'd jump to the top of the tall wooden fence and preen and pout well out of Finn's reach. Daddy Big Un liked to roughhouse with Finn. Finn would growl and howl and bounce and pounce until Daddy Big Un rubbed Finn's belly and, in a gulping breath (his chest going up and down), declare the game over and Finn the winner. Finn really adored the Big Uns: Mommy Big Un looked after Finn (and the Boy), and Daddy Big Un kept Finn occupied when the Boy wasn't home in the evening or at night. But Finn loved the Boy most of all. He loved the Boy more than basketball, more than dog cookies, more than anything in the whole wide Wold.

"A Lab's ears are made of *SILK*," the Boy whispered every night before falling asleep (unless the Boy was stuck in a Sleepover), and then one dark, dark night: the Boy didn't say it.

Finn paced the floor. He sniffed the Boy's socks for signs of sickness. He climbed on the bed and sat next to the Boy. The Boy didn't look sick. Sure, he looked older—the Boy smelled more and more like Daddy Big Un every day, but that wasn't a bad thing. Something *had* to be wrong though. Finn chewed on his fur and nibbled on the ear of a stuffed animal. He wandered downstairs to the family room and stared at the turtle's aquarium and the cage with the guinea pig, whom he rarely saw, just quivering whiskers sticking out of a shoebox. He poked his nose into the aquarium tank but, nope—no one home as usual, just a green rock that always seemed to be in a different place. He thought he heard his best friend, Sawyer, the cream-colored Lab who lived next door on the other side of the wooden fence, bark to him twice even though it was late (Sawyer was soft-spoken and not very gabby), but Finn didn't feel much like answering. Back upstairs, Finn pushed open the door at the end of the hall with his schnozz and stared at the Big Uns, but Daddy Big Un was snoring so loudly (he sounded like he had swallowed a cow!) that Mommy Big Un was clinging to the edge of the bed. Her mouth was open, and drool dripped to a puddle on the floor. The Big Uns wouldn't be able to help him.

Finn crawled back to the Boy's room, but he couldn't make himself climb next to the Boy. Finn curled into a ball on the floor at the foot of the bed instead. When he woke the next morning, the night's unpleasantness dissipated instantly like the nightmares he had sometimes about Alley Cat chasing *him* (as that one squirrel had). It wasn't until after the Boy had left for school that Finn remembered what had happened—and only because something else occurred: the Boy left without saying goodbye to Finn. The Boy *always* rubbed Finn's noggin before he left for school. "For luck," the Boy used to say, but he hadn't said that in quite some time. (It had taken Finn a while to get used to the phrase's absence, until Finn just started saying it to himself whenever the Boy pet his large head.) Finn had stationed himself near the door and had been sitting there for a good long time when Mommy Big Un came swooping by, heading up the stairs.

"He's gone already, Finn," Mommy Big Un said. "I have to vacuum, so skedaddle."

Finn bunkered beneath the kitchen table where he nibbled on a few stray Cheerios, trying to ignore Vacuum's noise. The only sound uglier than Vacuum's sucking *whoosh* was Alley Cat's singing. And if there was a sound uglier than Alley Cat's singing, Finn hoped he'd never hear it.

Finn lay low most of the day. Minutes were hours. At the appropriate time, Finn positioned himself by the front door (Finn couldn't really tell time as much as *feel* it), and Mommy Big Un chattered at him in words he didn't completely understand other than this: the Boy wasn't coming home directly from school.

Now Finn went through something like this at the end of every summer. He knew it was coming—the end of summer—just like you know school starts again on Monday, and thoughts of Monday drape a cloak over almost all of Sunday. It was like that. Every fall, Finn had to get used to a new routine and a day without the Boy running around in wet trunks and bare feet. This wasn't like fall though. This was different. During the school year, the Boy *always* came right home after his last class or activity. Finn's brain couldn't stop thinking of all the horrible things that could have befallen the Boy. Cars were fun to ride in, but they sometimes squished creatures just because they could; cars weren't completely domesticated. Maybe the Boy had been hunted down by a car. One time, last summer, some kids from around the corner had chased the Boy and tripped him, and the Boy fell on his face and cried, and the tears made designs in the dirt that had caked on his face. Finn made sure to snuggle up extra close that night. "Bullies," Mommy Big Un had said. Maybe the bullies (whom Finn imagined as being horned and hoofed) had trapped the Boy and were making him kiss the dirt *this very second*!

Finn didn't nap at all the rest of the afternoon. Every time he drifted off—about every fifteen minutes or so—he was jolted awake by images of the Boy in some sort of danger. Finn couldn't eat; he didn't want to pee. Mommy Big Un let him into his backyard Kingdom through the sliding glass door, but Finn mostly stayed on the patio near the entranceway in the shade of the dogwood tree, which was close enough to the house that he'd hear the Boy when he came home. When Alley Cat jumped on the top of the fence and sang in his trembling soprano, Finn covered his ears with his paws.

"Are you *d*ying, dog?" Alley Cat asked from a safe distance atop the tall wooden fence. Alley Cat looked like most of the other cats in the Wold to Finn: a fuzzy porridge mixture of grey and black and silver with jewels for eyes and switchblades for toes—except Alley Cat, although full grown, was only half the size of every other cat Finn had ever seen.

"What's '*d*ying'?" Finn asked back, his head flat on the patio stonework, the dogwood's boughs stirring above him.

"Buying the farm. Biting the dust. Pushing up daisies. Crossing over, essentially."

Finn didn't like the sound of these choices—especially the one about the farm. Finn thought that one was especially cruel-sounding.

"Are you sick then, dog?" Alley Cat asked.

"I don't think so," Finn replied, flicking his tongue to his nose.

"Depressed?"

Finn shook his head and sighed.

"Debilitated?"

Finn shrugged as best as a dog could shrug.

"Destroyed?"

Finn was getting annoyed, but not so much at Alley Cat—Alley Cat was *supposed* to be annoying. Finn was annoyed with himself. He had to have done something wrong to make the Boy stay away so long, to make the Boy forget about Finn's *SILK* and neglect Finn's noggin.

"De-feated," Alley Cat said as he sauntered away. "*Dis*-gusting."

And *d*isgusting, Finn thought, just about summed up how he felt. In truth, all of Alley Cat's *D* words seemed to describe perfectly the hollowed-out sensation filling Finn's barrel chest. When Daddy Big Un came home—Finn knew it was Daddy Big Un because the Boy didn't drive a car—the Big Uns sat down at the table and ate dinner together—no Boy! No one sneaked a piece of bread or a slice of apple under the table for Finn. No one rubbed his back with their toes.

When the Boy (finally) arrived home, Finn forgot all of his *d*espair—there was a *D* word Alley Cat had left out!—and leapt on him, smacking the floor with his wagging tail, licking the Boy's hands and face when he leaned down to untie his shoelaces.

"Hey Finn," the Boy said before heading upstairs.

Finn bounded after him.

The Boy walked into his room—and closed the door.

Finn was *d*evastated. Finn was *d*emolished. Finn was *d*ismissed.

Later, when Mommy Big Un yelled up the stairs that "the phone's for you—it's a *girrrrrllllll*," the Boy opened the door, stepped over Finn, and stood in the Big Uns' room talking into the receiver. (He wasn't allowed to have a cell phone yet—something he complained about often to Finn.)

"…Mr. Colton was *so* mean…I know!…can't read all those chapters in one week…"

Finn crept into the Boy's room and sniffed the blankets on the bed. Nope—Finn hadn't peed there by accident. He poked his head under the Boy's desk—the Boy must have been sitting there because books were open and the seat of his chair smelled warm—no, no pee or poop there either. Not that Finn really thought he'd peed or pooped in the Boy's room—Finn never had any accidents—but he had to have done *something*.

"…right…and then the pop quiz on top of that…"

Maybe if Finn brought the Boy his shoes. For some reason, Daddy Big Un had once spent an entire afternoon trying to get Finn to bring him a pair of slippers. Finn fetched them all day long and everyone seemed pretty happy with him. They gave Finn lots of cookies, but no one ever asked him to fetch the slippers again. Finn thought that maybe he was supposed to fetch them on his own, but soon the whole slipper incident was a just a little memory in his big noggin.

Maybe that was it! Maybe the Boy wanted Finn to get his shoes!

"...sure, that would be cool...I'll ask my mom..."

Finn snatched the Boy's shoes—the ones the Boy wore to church—and stood in the hallway. He wanted to peek in the Big Uns' room, where the Boy paced as he spoke on the phone, but in the end, Finn decided that surprise was best. The Boy would be so happy!

"...yeah, no, well, I like you too..."

Of course, what happened next would haunt Finn for a long, long time. You know the cliché: the straw that broke the camel's back? Well, Finn had never seen a camel, and a cliché was completely foreign to him, but deep beneath his black fur, inside Little White Tie, camels were breaking down into tiny little pieces, and as Finn well knew from listening to the Boy read aloud, all the king's horses and all the king's men could never put the broken camel together again. Or something like that.

The Boy hung up the phone, and Finn noticed that his face was pink and he could smell that the Boy was sweaty—not sweaty like he'd been running around the backyard playing basketball with Finn; this was a different kind of sweaty. It wasn't a sick sweaty either. The Boy was smiling. And Finn thought the smiles were for him. He let the shoes drop from his mouth. He wagged his tail like he was trying to sweep the floor and puffed out his chest, waiting for the Boy to notice.

And, *woo wee!*, did the Boy notice! At first Finn couldn't figure out why the Boy's face went from sweaty pink to angry red. Finn had seen the Big Uns paint their faces this color before, but not the Boy, not often anyway, and *never* directed at Finn.

"BAD DOG!" the Boy yelled.

Debased.

Degenerate.

Dead weight.

Finn looked down. Where there had been shoes, there were only two piles of crunchy black leather. Finn flicked his tongue around his mouth and spit out another little piece.

D words crowded inside his slowly *d*iminishing chest.

The Boy yelled again.

Mommy Big Un yelled more.

(It must be said—and Finn thought this much, much later—that the Boy and Mommy Big Un, who were angry, were nothing like the Yellers from his First House, who yelled simply because they were mean, perhaps even hateful, but Finn at the moment was having a hard time telling the difference.)

Daddy Big Un didn't yell, but he ignored Finn, and Finn crept behind the sofa and stayed there even after lights-out, licking his paws, crying softly to himself.

*D*is-gusted.

The next day, Finn was determined to be on his best behavior. Daddy Big Un stepped over Finn with a barely a grunt, but that was nothing unusual for morning time. Mommy Big Un let Finn out for his morning pee, then gave him a cookie when he came in. All normal. Finn didn't want the cookie—he didn't feel he deserved one—but he ate it anyway. It had been a long night behind the sofa.

Finn didn't quite remember what he'd done to feel so bad—it is the peculiar curse of dogs: to be unable to let go of the emotion, but to not always recall *exactly* how they came to feel that way. One thing was for sure: when the Boy came down for breakfast, Finn would be ready for him.

It took Finn a minute or two to rustle up his basketball. He found it behind Daddy Big Un's recliner, and a spider—probably Ms. Silk—had started spinning a web from the surface of the ball to the back of the chair. Just pushing at the basketball with his nose—which was running, by the way, running like it was in a hurry but had no place to go—made Finn's Little White Tie heavy and sad. When the tiny web stretched and snapped and broke apart, Finn thought he understood what Ms. Silk might feel when she returned home and found it gone.

Finn set himself up at the bottom of the stairs, sat straight up so the Boy would see Little White Tie, and held the basketball between his big jaws. There was little time to reflect on pettings past, but if ever a dog needed one...

The Boy came down the stairs—and walked *around* Finn.

This wasn't good. No noggin rubs. No, "Morning, Finn!" Finn ran after the Boy and dropped the basketball at his moving feet.

"Not now, Finn," the Boy said, kicking the basketball into the family room.

Ahh! Here we go! Finn tore after the orange-and-blue-striped basketball. The Boy would be so happy to see how fast he retrieved it!

But when he returned, the Boy was already sitting in the kitchen with the Big Uns, concentrating on a bowl of crunchies. Finn sat in the kitchen doorway, tail wagging, drool gathering around the ball.

Nothing.

Finn dropped the basketball and pushed it towards the Boy with his black nose.

Absolutely nothing.

Finally, in a move that Finn would later severely chastise himself for, he opened up his huge mouth and let it all out: the frustration and the sadness and the confusion and the *D* words, but most of all: the love—Finn's crushing love for the Boy.

WOOF!

WOOF!

WOOF!

WOOF!

WOOF!

WOOF!

WOOF!

And the Boy was woofing back! Little White Tie leapt like a cold frog on a hot stone.

But what the Boy was saying was: "Out, Finn! Now! Get out!"

Get out?

"That was an expensive pair of shoes," said Mommy Big Un.

And then Finn remembered what he had done.

That night, the Boy was late coming home again, but the Big Uns didn't seem worried. Finn did all the worrying, thank you. He paced and cried a little (to himself) and gnawed his way through a bone that should have lasted him a month. When the Boy finally walked through the door, Mommy Big Un was already in bed reading a book. (Finn had checked on her several times to make sure she hadn't sneaked out to pick up the Boy.) Daddy Big Un, who'd been lounging downstairs in his pajamas, patted the Boy on the back and told him to get some rest.

Finn followed the Boy upstairs and lay outside the bathroom peeking. The Boy was staring at himself in the mirror. He ran a finger over his upper lip and then pursed both of them—that was when Finn noticed the Boy's lips were redder than usual. The Boy kissed the mirror. Finn buried his snout in his paws.

When he lifted his noggin again, the bathroom light was out and the Boy's bedroom door was closed.

No bedtime stories or Blue Books.

No sharing a pillow with Finn.

No reminders about Finn's *SILK* ears.

Finn crept back behind the sofa.

He heard Sawyer bark once but it was abruptly cut short, which was fitting because Finn was starting to feel cut off and alone.

When the next day was a repeat of the day before, Finn knew it was time to go. Although he didn't recall much about his First House, home of the Yellers, Finn knew at least that there had *been* a First House. So there could be a Third House somewhere.

How could this have happened if my ears are made of *SILK*, Finn wanted to know. How?

Although Finn didn't know exactly what this phrase meant—he'd heard the Big Uns use it and it felt right—Finn thought he would just buy the farm when he was packing his things, especially when he realized he didn't have many *things*. The food and water bowls were his, of course, but they proved too unwieldy to bring along. There were his stuffed animals too. Finn loved his stuffed animals. He used to pretend *he* was the Boy and that the monkey or the frog or the elephant or the panda was him! Finn knew he'd miss those games and miss his guys, Monkey and Frog and Elephant and Panda, but in the end, the orange-and-blue-striped basketball was the only thing Finn took with him—besides his fanciful imagination.

How come no one remembers that my ears are made of SILK?

Finn walked around the house one last time, avoiding any reflections. He didn't want to know what *d*evastation looked like. It was bad enough to feel it. It was bad enough that *D* words were inside of him, settling in, getting comfortable, muffling Little White Tie.

What if the Boy had lied?

What if my ears aren't made of SILK *after all?*

Finn took one look behind him and scooped the ball up.

He'd find out. He'd seek out the wise and the learned. If his ears were truly made of *SILK*, Finn thought, then he would be worth more than an expensive pair of shoes. And if that was true, then maybe he could sell his ear flaps and buy the Boy new shoes and once again be allowed to fall asleep next to him, counting all of the Boy's heartbeats, waking with his noggin buried beneath the Boy's blankets.

And if my ears aren't *made of* SILK?

He had to find the answer.

For some reason the patio door had been left partially open. Was this a sign? Finn approached the opening, shuddered, and took the first of many steps into the outside Wold.

Episode II

What Pig Said

It didn't take long for Finn to become lost—in his head anyway. The outside Wold was new and scary, and Finn had little experience in it. He had no idea how long he'd been walking, but it seemed like forever. Finally he saw a partially open sliding glass door off a stone patio; someone must not have closed it all the way. He squeezed himself and his basketball through the opening and crept inside for shelter. When he finally rested, he made sure to keep one eye on his basketball; Finn didn't want anyone stealing it away.

"ACHOO!"

Finn woke in a fit—one second he was playing basketball with the Boy and eating all the cookies he wanted, and the next, he was shivering from the cold. The basketball had rolled away a bit, but Finn was able to retrieve it easily with his paws.

"ACHOO!"

Finn sat up.

"Ga-blesh-you," Finn said.

"Thank ye."

Finn sniffed the air. Even though he couldn't see the sneezer, there was a familiar smell.

"Do I know you?"

"ACHOO!"

"Ga-blesh-you again," Finn said.

"Thank ye again," the voice responded.

Sniffle, sniffle.

"Where are you?" Finn asked.

Cough, cough.

Finn decided it might be time to move on.

"Excuse me, mister," Finn said. "Do you know of any place I could go that isn't so cold?"

"Ye were sleeping on the vent," the voice said.

Finn turned around. True enough! He *had* been sleeping on a vent. A steady, cold breeze blasted from the floor. Finn started to lift himself from the vent, but it wasn't easy—the only parts of him still asleep were his hind legs and rear end!

"No, no—don't move. Ye were blocking it quite nicely."

Finn sat back down.

"Where are you?" Finn asked again, looking around, even studying the carpet.

"Up here, heathen," the voice said. "How many times do we have to go over this?"

Finn looked up, and there to his left, inside a large cage on a shelf, just at Finn's eye level, was Pig. The cage had a round food bowl plus a water bottle suspended from one side. There was an upside down shoebox on the far right. On the other side of the cage were two grey cardboard toilet paper rolls. Pig was brown and white and black and looked like a chubby log of fur with two little, round, pink ears stuck on one end. He was huddled beneath a blanket of cedar chips and newspapers. Pig appeared to possess a nervous habit: he nibbled on his own whiskers.

"Mr. Guinea Pig!" Finn cried. "How did you get here?"

"Careful," Pig said, sniffling.

Finn cocked his head.

"Of what?"

"Ye are breathing on me."

Finn lowered his noggin and tried to breathe on something else.

"I am sorry, Mr. Pig."

"I could catch cold, ye know," Pig sniffed.

Finn was familiar with fetching things. "What would you do with it if you caught it?"

"It's not like catching a ball or a stick, dog," Pig said with a hint of venom in his voice. "It's a *cold*."

"A cold," Finn repeated, sniffling himself.

"Coughing," Pig said. "Sneezing."

"Hmm," Finn said, still not sure, but not wanting to be rude.

"Like hairballs," Pig offered.

"Oh," Finn said, for he knew the danger of hairballs (although they were more of a cat thing, as he understood it).

Pig coughed a little. He sucked on his whiskers.

"I could *die*, ye know."

"*Die?*"

"Yes, *die*: *morte*. Deleted. Ceasing to exist. Dead. Crossing over."

"*Die*," Finn said, trying out the new *D* word. It didn't sound so good in his mouth; either did "crossing over," and there weren't even any *d*'s in the phrase.

"*Die*," Finn said again, but this time he said it more softly to see if that made him feel any better. It didn't. "*Die*" sounded gloomy even when he just *thought* the word.

"From a cold," Pig said. "Cavies do that. *Die* from a cold."

"That sure does sound awful, Mr. Pig," Finn said. He still wasn't sure what "*die*" meant, but Pig certainly seemed upset enough about it.

"Cavy," Pig said.

"Ga-blesh-you again," Finn said.

"I didn't sneeze."

"But you...I—"

"Cavy. *I'm* a cavy," Pig said, chewing on his whiskers. "Of the genus *Cavia* in the family *caviidae*. To call me a guinea pig is an insult to my race."

"I don't know about any of that, Mr. Pig, sir, and I'm sorry," Finn said, "but I'm on a Great Journey of sorts, and I was wondering if you could help me."

"And why should I?" Pig said, so upset he flipped off his newspaper blanket and walked into his food bowl. "A cavy helping a black Labrador retriever? Whoever heard of such nonsense? Besides—what about that time ye barked at me."

"I don't remember, but I am truly sorry if I did. Sometimes I bark just because. Maybe you scared me."

"Oh, so it's my fault?" Pig asked.

Pig noticed he had four whiskers stuck in his mouth, and, as casually as a chubby guinea pig could, he noisily hacked the whiskers out (along with a fair amount of lime-green phlegm) and nibbled on a toilet paper roll. ("To cleanse the palate.")

"Besides: my title is Vicar," Pig said, briefly lifting himself on a toilet paper roll and puffing out his round tummy. "I'm a Vicar to ye. I've also been called a Cleric and sometimes an Ecclesiastic, but Vicar has a better sound." As an aside: "I really should look it up one of these days, if I haven't peed on the...on the..."

"Dictionary," Finn added, just to be helpful. (The Boy had the beast with two names—Merriam and Webster—on his desk.) Finn realized with a start that "dictionary" was a *D* word, although perhaps not as *d*angerous.

Pig ignored him, murmuring to himself, whistling through his teeth. "He can't hear me if I whisper. I'm not a dog whistle, after all." But Finn could hear every word; guinea pigs are notoriously bad whisperers. Only piebald veiled chameleons and rhinos were worse, and most dogs can't whisper at all including Labs.

One of Pig's whiskers flickered in the huffing and puffing and went up his nose.

"ACHOO!"

Finn refrained himself from bleshing Pig.

"Ordained and everything. Nondenominational, of course. Inclusive *and* intolerant. But no matter the faith, I am the Vicar." Pig said. "I earned the title, and for that alone, I deserve your respect. I don't have to do anything else."

More quietly: "It was through a mail order course, but still...."

Oh my, this isn't going well, Finn thought, and he stood up and yawned, more out of sheer frustration than sleepiness—although, Finn *was* still very tired, despite his nap. He almost always needed an after-nap after a nap.

Pig scurried behind his water bottle and shivered and shoved as many whiskers in his mouth as he could.

"Please, don't hurt me," Pig said, trembling. "Don't."

Finn sat back down.

"Hurt you? I would never do that."

Pig stopped shaking and looked abashed.

"Heightened sense of fear," Pig said, not looking at Finn. "My yoke to bear."

"I just wanted to ask—"

"Are ye saved?" Pig asked first, now staring Finn straight in the eyes.

"Saved?"

Pig tossed his nose in the air, as much to illustrate the importance of his point—being saved!—as to dislodge a stray whisker still stuck between his teeth.

"Saved!"

"From who?" Finn asked, looking around.

Momentarily distracted when the stray whisker *sprung* back into place, Pig muttered: "Truth be told, I picked up that word—saved—from one of the newspapers in my abode. I also know 'enlightenment,' but I can't spell it."

It was well known that guinea pigs were terrible spellers but were pretty good at arithmetic; they just couldn't count on their toes, as they only had four on each front foot or paw and three on each of their back ones.

"Where was I?" Pig said.

"You asked if I was—"

"I remember—don't get your collar in a twist! *Ahem.* I was asking: are ye going to go to the Goodly Place, boyo, or are ye going to…the Other Place?"

Finn looked behind him and shuddered as a shadow crossed the room. Was Alley Cat slinking about? If so, however did the cat find him?

"Well, I'm not quite sure *where* I'm going," Finn said. "I've been wandering around for—"

"Looks like ye haven't even left the house, dog," Pig said dismissively.

"I haven't?"

"Ye don't go to the Goodly Place or the Other Place until ye leave the house, if ye get my drift. Until the Lordy calls ye," Pig said. "The Big Uns will lie to ye. They'll tell ye, 'Come on, let's go for a ride, dog,' and suddenly ye find yourself at the vet's and the next thing ye know: SQUEAK—ye are gaspin' for air; ye are clawin' the sky. Then ye meet the Lordy."

"Who is the Lordy?" Finn asked, genuinely curious and wanting to change the subject from all the gaspin' and clawin'. (Besides, he liked his vet.)

Pig sputtered and spit and turned in a circle. His whiskers were all askew, as if they'd exploded on his face. Finn sniffed at the cage in concern. Perhaps all the whisker sucking had made Pig confused about his place in the Wold—more confused than Finn.

"Ye don't know who the Lordy is?" Pig asked.

"I don't know…I was just…I don't think we've met."

"He is the Vet of all Vets!"

Finn definitely did *not* want to meet the Vet of all Vets. His vet was a nice man who always gave him a cookie for his troubles, but whenever he went to see him, Finn got a shot in the rump. Once he tried to make a run for it and jumped from the exam table, but Daddy Big Un and the lady named Tech, who always smelled like coconut (so yummy!), scooped him up, and he got shot after all.

"Do ye, um, congregate with cats?" Pig asked in a casual tone.

"Cats? No, Mr. Pig—Mr. Vicar, sir. I chase Alley Cat once in a while."

Pig lowered his voice to a whisper (or as close as he could get).

"Fine, fine. Can't get into the Goodly Place consorting with cats."

"Consorting?"

Finn tried to put all of his energy into his Smart Bump, which all Labrador retrievers have on the back of their noggins, but suddenly his bump didn't seem so bright, and he thought that maybe he should ask what "consorting" meant lest he put his paw in it, but he didn't have to.

Pig shook his head, his whiskers swishing back and forth. "To consort is to associate, to accompany, to chum with. Get thee a lexicon, Lab."

Finn thought the word "chum" sounded familiar, but he didn't remember from where. He was embarrassed that he didn't know what a lexicon was, though even if he did, he wouldn't be able to read it since dogs, generally, don't know how to read. But he was so anxious to get to his question, words like "lexicon" and "chum" seemed to go in one ear and out the other.

"Vicar, I was wondering, that is, if I may ask—"

"My title, dog, is Prelate...or is Praetor? I forget." Finn's eyes went wide as Pig tried to stand on his hind legs but ended up plopping unceremoniously on his bed of cedar chips and torn newspaper. "It's from Latin anyway."

Latin, Finn thought, sounded delicious. It reminded him of the pieces of crunchy taco shells and soft tortilla bread that the Boy used to sneak to him under the table in better times.

"As long as ye sit at my feet, disciple, ye may call me Vicar."

Tamales!

Drip, drip, drip.

There was more embarrassment when Finn discovered he was drooling all over his basketball—and not paying attention to the Vicar.

"Do ye like girls?" Pig asked. "Ye have to like girls to get into the Goodly Place."

"I wasn't trying to get into *any* place. I just wanted to know if my—"

"Ye like girls then, dog?"

Finn thought for a moment. Pig had thrown a lot of information at him. Finn did have a girlfriend, but she was more of a friend who was a girl than anything else, though she was very affectionate.

"Well..." Finn began carefully, making sure he used the right words, watching Pig's little face. (Finn loved how his nose never stopped twitching!). "I love the Boy."

Pig squeaked (and turned round and round).

Pig squealed (and turned round some more).

Pig sounded like this: WHEEET! WHEEET! WHEEET!

Finn tried to not look surprised, but the Pig's song was so high-pitched! Finn's ears quivered and quavered.

Pig's circle dance came to a halt in a flurry of dust and chips.

"HACK!"

From Pig's mouth came another tiny pile of green-tinted stuff: bits of newspaper and toilet paper roll, small pieces of what Finn assumed had been Pig's lunch, and there, stuck standing in the center of the pile: a trembling stalk of translucent white. Pig had swallowed one of his own whiskers!

The cavy ignored the evidence and, unwisely, attempted another circle dance.

"Ye love a boy?" Pig asked in a husky tone after coming to an unsteady standstill.

"Don't you?" Finn asked in return. "Don't you love a Boy—or a Girl?"

Pig turned his back to Finn.

"Ye will *never* get into the Goodly Place if ye love a boy," Pig said. "I'm the Vicar. I know! It's been *d*emonstrated."

*D*emonstrated.

"It's been *d*emonized," Pig continued, turning around.

*D*emonized.

"The Goodly Book says, 'He who consorts with a boy will forthwith be *d*efiled.' Or something like that."

*D*efiled.

Finn tried to remember all the Blue Books the Boy had read to him. They were all Goodly Books as far as Finn was concerned. In the Blue Books, the two brothers were always solving mysteries. There certainly seemed to be a lot of love between the boys. It struck him that maybe the Vicar wasn't very nice, but he stayed on his best behavior nonetheless.

Pig was still talking: "If ye don't accept the Lordy into your heart, dog, ye will not go to the Goodly Place, where dog cookies are served all the livelong day, no indeed; ye will go somewhere hot as heck."

Finn spoke before he thought: "I wasn't going to the Goodly Place." (Even though unlimited cookies sounded mighty fine!) "I was looking for someone to—"

Pig scampered right up to the side of his cage.

"What d'ye do?" Pig asked, salivating a little, seemingly anxious for details. "If ye aren't going to the Goodly Place, ye had to have done *something*," he said.

"Lie? Tell a whopper?" Pig asked.

"Steal, perhaps?" Pig suggested.

"Did ye—did ye *murder* someone?" Pig gasped.

"Murder?" Finn asked, genuinely puzzled

Pig's heavy breathing was loud, and his breath smelled like hay.

"If ye did," Pig panted, "ye have to tell me everything."

"I…no…I never… I'm not even sure what that word means," Finn admitted, though it felt like a *D* word, such as *d*estruction or *d*eath, words he'd heard before though he didn't know their meanings.

"Are ye a Christian then? They're some goodly folks, I think. I'd be one if I wasn't already a…a… Well, are ye?"

Finn tuned Pig out, as he tried to choose the right words before answering, since there was no telling what would set off the Vicar…or was it Prelate?

"Well…I don't know what one is, to be honest, sir. But I am a retriever. Throw something," Finn said to be helpful, "and I'll bring it right back real, real fast." He was actually eager to chase after something; it had been a while.

Pig shook his head. "Some Christians, ye know, have something called Confession. So is that what it is, dog? Did ye confess your *d*astardly *d*eed already? Have ye been forgiven, and if so, for *wha*?"

Thinking of the Boy's shoes, it was now Finn's turn to shake his head.

"So probably not a Christian. How 'bout a Jain? A Buddhist maybe? They're an okay bunch, although very quiet."

"I've actually never heard of those either, Mr. Vicar, sir."

Finn was eyeing Pig's water bottle. He was pretty thirsty from all his travelling and all this talking.

"Focus, my child," Pig said.

Finn tried but found himself thinking of the puddle he'd passed in a backyard on his way to the patio—he was that thirsty!—the puddle that looked just like the one in his (former) backyard Kingdom. (It had rained the night before in his part of town too.)

Pig shrank back.

"Ye are not a Sikh, are ye?" he asked before quickly composing himself. "Not that there's anything wrong with that; I just can never remember how to spell it, so that makes me afraid. I'm afraid of a great many *other* religions, some of which I can spell quite easily, like Muslim. So...are ye a Sikh or a Muslim or a—?"

"No, I'm—"

"Jewish? A Hindu?"

Finn's head was spinning. All of these words were unfamiliar to him, as they are to most Labrador retrievers—most dogs for that matter.

Pig stamped one of his little feet (which Finn thought would have been awfully funny if things hadn't turned so serious). The cavy coughed and out came a cloud of hay dust.

"Ga-blesh-you," Finn said.

"Salt lick and a biscuit!" Pig squeaked. "Will ye *please* stop bleshing?"

"I'm sorry, Mr. Vicar, sir. Like I said before, I'm on a Great Journey. I'm looking for an answer."

Pig showed Finn his butt, considered a sign of disrespect by guinea pigs (but not dogs).

"All the answers ye need are in the Goodly Book of Goodly Things," Pig said.

"The Goodly Book of...Goodly Things? Well, where can I find the...?"

Pig turned around slowly (he had to; Pig was portly) and eyeballed Finn.

"I'm saved," Pig said proudly, puffing his chest out. "For I am the conduit of the Lordy."

Finn tried not to giggle. Pig's chest was *so* little compared to his.

"The era of subtlety is over!" Pig declared.

"Ask me!" Pig challenged. "I've read the Goodly Book of Goodly Things backwards and forwards. I know sin and I know our Lordy. In fact, I know the Lordies of all religions. Ask me, canine."

Finn looked down at his paws, embarrassed. The moment was here, finally here. Finn raised his noggin and brought his nose close to the bars of the cage. Pig backed up a wee bit.

"Are my ears made of *SILK*?" Finn asked.

"WHEET! WHEET! WHEET!" went the cavy.

"That's your question?" Pig's eyes bulged like two tiny, black basketballs. "That's the question ye bring to someone of my stature? I'm *enlightened*, ye know. Oh yes, not every Vicar—or was it Proctor?—is enlightened. Mix a pinch of the east into the west. The Goodly Book of Goodly Things *and* the Pawpath Sutra. WHEET! WHEET! WHEET! I've meditated and I've prayed. I've laid down— for my kind cannot sit in the lotus position or kneel—and nibbled quietly while thinking deep thoughts that were, *ahem*, very deep indeed. I've walked around my cage—for we are all in a cage, dog— contemplating, reflecting, and, well, nibbling. WHEET! WHEET! WHEET! All this I know and all this I've done, and ye ask me about your *ears*?"

"Yes," Finn said; he was making (a little) progress. "I need to know if my ears are really made of *SILK*."

"Sit, please, dog," Pig said. "The *d*raft."

Finn sat down upon the cold vent. It was rather unpleasant.

"I told ye: if I catch cold, I'll *d*ie," Pig said.

"What's '*d*ie' again?" Finn asked. Now he had two questions!

"Kicking the bucket. Giving up the ghost. Sleeping the big sleep."

Finn titled his head. He didn't understand.

"No. More. Carrots," Pig sighed while saying each word slowly.

"I don't really like carrots," Finn said.

"Then ye won't mind takin' my place," Pig exclaimed, jumping up (but not very high, as guinea pigs—cavies—generally don't jump, although they've been known to hop).

"That's it!" Pig said, trying to snap his little fingers. "Ye can take my place!"

"Take your place?"

"Yes, yes. I'll tell ye if your ears are made of *SILK*, and ye can take my place."

Finn eyed the cavy's cage.

"I don't think I'd fit," Finn said. "I'm grown."

Pig muttered to himself and kicked his food bowl with the crooked toes of his right back paw.

"Darn it all to heck, ye are right, dog," Pig said to himself, as he fluffed the torn newspapers and cedar chips together to make a bed. "Gosh darn Darwin. Gotta stick with the Goodly Book, gotta follow the Pawpath," he muttered, shivering.

Finn gestured with his black nose (which was a bit runny, probably because of the vent) towards the upside down shoebox.

"If you're cold, why don't you sleep in there?" Finn asked. "It's gotta be warmer than those old newspapers, Mr. Vicar."

"The Lordy will provide," Pig said.

"Provide what?" Finn asked. "And which Lordy?"

"Speak up," Pig said, clearly irritated. "I don't speak 'dog' all that well."

"The Lordy will provide you with what?" Finn asked. Personally he hoped it was some dog cookies—which he would share, of course—for his tummy was rumbling.

"Shelter. The Wold's a mess. Goin' to pieces. Just look at these headlines," Pig said, gesturing to his shredded newspapers.

"You peed on that one," Finn said. "It's all smeared."

Pig shuffled the newspapers with his back paws.

"A-ha! See!" Pig shouted—then grew quiet. "Oh. The funny pages. Never mind. What the Vicar does is bring all these things together under the...under the...under the protection of the Blanket of the Lordy!"

Finn waited what he thought was an appropriate amount of time, then spoke very quietly: "Why are you afraid of *d*ying?"

Pig managed (sort of) another jump and hit his nose on the bars of his cage.

"Why? *Why?*" Pig asked. "WHEET! WHEET! WHEET! Because when we *d*ie—well, when *I d*ie—when whoever *d*ies—the Lordy judges ye according to how ye have lived your life. If ye were good and followed the Goodly Book of Goodly Things and stayed clear of the others and the infidels and the cats—especially the cats!—then ye get into the Goodly Place. No cages in the Goodly Place! No aquariums! And no colds! Just ye and others like ye—or, rather, me and others like me."

"But why are you afraid?" Finn asked, more confused than before.

"They let hamsters in now, I heard," Pig sniffed.

"The spotted ones?" Finn had seen a spotted cat once, and it terrified him.

"Oh, yes. Black mice and purple ferrets too, even brown gerbils."

"Purple...mice?" Finn asked, a tad confused.

"Black! *Black mice!* Lordy on a soda cracker! Ye are a *black* Lab, for goodness sakes!"

Finn thrust his chest out.

"I have a Little White Tie."

Pig gasped. "Mixin' the races!"

Finn sighed.

"Mr. Vicar, sir, I'm not looking for this Goodly Place or any place. I'm looking for an answer to my very important question."

Finn thought of all the books with the blue covers on the Boy's bookshelf. "It's...it's more of a mystery," Finn said.

"A mystery?" Pig asked, looking interested.

Finally!

"Yes, yes!" Finn said, still thinking of the Blue Books. "The Mystery of the *SILK* Ears!"

Pig waddled away from the side of his cage. "Back to that," he said, distrust in his squeaky voice. "Back to the ears. Do ye think *my* ears are made of *SILK*?" Pig suddenly demanded. "Do ye?"

"I wouldn't know, Mr. Vicar, sir. I'm not even sure what *SILK* is," Finn admitted. "Except I know what it looks like in my head. It looks like this."

And Finn thought really, really hard and used his Smart Bump and conjured everything he knew about *SILK* and everything he loved about the Boy:

SILK...

The Boy's soft hands...

SILK...

The Boy's breathing when he was asleep...

"I can't see inside your head, dog," Pig said. "But I can tell ye this: if your kind values ears of this sort, then ye should strive to have those kinds of ears. The price of *SILK* is not cheap! And, if ye are able to attain this state of *SILK*, don't be afraid to flaunt it. For if ye do have *SILK* ears, then the Lordy surely blessed your protrusions, son, even though ye are from the *Canis familiaris* species. But ye need to make sure no one else takes your *SILK* from ye, understand? Ye need to be willin' to die for it, and for certain, ye need to make sure others—and there will be plenty of 'em, others without this *SILK*— ye need to make sure they know they will burn for not believing in *your SILK*. Or at least make sure they feel inferior. See, dog: they'll kill ye for your *SILK*. Remember this: who made *SILK*? The Lordy made *SILK*."

But Finn had already lifted his bottom from the grate on the floor and retrieved his basketball. Pig made him uncomfortable. It was go. Time to continue his quest. (He heard a single familiar bark coming from somewhere outside.) More than anything, Finn wanted to go home, curl up next to the Boy, and let all of Pig's nasty words escape in a snore or two.

"Don't ye walk away from me and leave me in the *d*raft," Pig squealed, diving into his shoebox. "WHEET! WHEET! I'll pray for ye, dog! Ye will burn too if I don't! WHEET! WHEET!"

Finn was tempted, just a little, to bark and growl and generally throw a gala fit, but Finn knew finding the truth about *SILK* was more important than scaring Pig. Besides: this Lordy that Pig spoke of sounded like he would know the answer (even if Pig himself was chock full of bile and chewed toilet paper rolls and misplaced whiskers). Pig's Lordy had to know what Finn's ears were worth. But where to find this Lordy? Finn left the way he came without looking back, remembering to take his basketball. Maybe he'd seek out Mr. Turtle, who was far older and surely had more wisdom than the Vicar.

"The way is narrow, dog," Pig squeaked, "and so our minds have to be too! Don't forget! Narrow is as narrow does!"

And that was what Pig said.

Episode III

What Sawyer Said

At first Finn ran from the Vicar. Once he felt he'd put enough distance between him and the Pig, he walked and walked, trying to keep off the beaten paths, which was difficult for almost all the paths were covered with tracks. He passed things that he thought he recognized while other things, seen from different perspectives, seemed new and odd. When he reached the hole in the wooden fence behind the shed, he heard the familiar bark again—just a single bark. Sawyer! Finn pushed himself through the hole, and even though it was small, the wood was old and gave easily. Finn wondered if the Mites had been eating it like they'd been eating at the fence and shed in his old yard. Daddy Big Un, once he discovered them, had said, "Well, there goes the neighborhood. They'll eat us out of house and home." Finn had thought this was terrible news. He stayed up all night (well, as best he could) hoping to catch the Mites eating the house—or was it the home? Finn wondered which of those he lived in. (Thank heavens he didn't live in the shed!) The next morning, the house (or the home) was intact and everyone went about their normal morning activities. To be sure, Finn peeked through the gate, and the neighborhood was still there. Daddy Big Un must have meant another neighborhood—maybe this one, which seemed somewhat familiar yet still strange.

After he went through the hole (pushing his orange-and-blue-striped basketball ahead of him with his nose), Finn shook as if he were wet and said to the air around him, "Please, Mites. Don't like the taste of dog."

An infinitesimal dot spoke to him from the fence. "Why, Finn, we've never eaten you before. Why would we start now?" It sounded like King Mite, but that couldn't be (just like he couldn't be on the edge of Sawyer's lawn). Maybe he was dreaming, he thought.

"How did you get over here, your majesty?" Finn asked.

"I'm roughly in the same place I'm always in, pooch. Did you get hit on the head?"

Finn was confused, but he bowed his noggin to the King (out of respect). Maybe there was more than one King Termite just like there seemed to be a hole in the fence that appeared to be the same size as the one behind the Big Uns' shed. One thing was for sure: he was in Sawyer's yard, his Kingdom, which (normally) was right next door to his. Maybe Sawyer's Big Uns had moved. Regardless, boy, was he ever glad to see his best buddy!

Other dogs called him the Sniffer, and true to form, there was Sawyer, standing in the middle of his yard with his snout in the air. Finn couldn't smell anything out of place, but Sawyer could smell a fire from three towns over (or so it was said). One thing was for sure: Sawyer's nose was never wrong. It was pink and there was a smattering of freckles near the top. But that wasn't the most unique thing about Sawyer. No, the most unique-looking thing about Sawyer was his color.

"Hi Finn!" Sawyer said without turning around, his tail going a million miles a minute. Sawyer was a good friend, Finn's best friend, in fact. Finn usually called him Tommy, which was his first name.

Sawyer's nose was still in the air, sniffing.

"Achoo!"

"Blesh you," Finn said cautiously. Pig had made him a tad reticent when it came to bleshing. But Sawyer was the sneeziest dog Finn ever knew.

Finn looked around: Sawyer's yard was filled with wall-to-wall dandelions! Finn remembered there being a few in the Big Uns' yard but nothing like this. Sawyer had a thing for dandelions, and he insisted upon smelling each one. Finn wasn't sure how his friend remembered which dandelions he'd already smelled, but this never appeared to be a concern for Sawyer, who had such respect for the little weed with the yellow flower that he tried not to pee or poop on them, if he could. During dandelion season (which apparently was still going on), Sawyer seemed to keep count of his yellow little friends. It was as if he was on a mission of sorts.

Maybe Sawyer would know if Finn's ears were made of *SILK*! He had another question now too (after all of Pig's talk of *dying*), but Finn didn't want to disturb his friend's sniffing.

With his nose still in the air, Sawyer pointed with one leg towards the old, rundown garage. It had been there for years, before the current house was even built, according to what Sawyer heard his

Big Uns say. There was a driveway, but it was outside the yard. Sawyer also heard that the garage used to be bright white, but now only dirty white chips in random spots remained.

"What is it?" Finn asked moving alongside his friend in case they needed to present a united front.

"Pirates," Sawyer said, and Finn was instantly both excited (Sawyer always planned the best adventures) and a little apprehensive (maybe there were really pirates hiding in the old garage among what Sawyer told him were tatty lawn chairs, old lamps, retired bicycles, and golf clubs that had grown rust-colored beards and never spoke when spoken to).

The Sniffer's snout tilted.

"Wait, please, Finn," he said before he tore through the weeds alongside the far fence. There, nibbling away, was Echo the grey rabbit. When Sawyer started running, Echo stayed absolutely still, but his little nose kept twitching, and at the last possible second, the rabbit broke from the weeds, Sawyer hot on his fluffy tail, and dove beneath the garage! Sawyer walked the perimeter quickly; there was no way for him to squeeze beneath the old garage. Now, there was no bad blood between Sawyer and Echo. During the last dog days of summer, they had both lain in the shade—on opposite sides of the yard—and Sawyer always made a point of asking after Echo's family, which took some time, as the rabbit's clan was quite large. But instinct and perhaps conditioning had made them partners in a decidedly not *d*angerous dance. Now, Finn enjoyed chasing the occasional bunny (who'd run under the shed) and had even gone after Echo a few times (if it was indeed the same Echo), but more because he felt it was expected of him than anything else. He really didn't have much time for chasing bunnies at the moment; he had to keep an eye out for Alley Cat, for he wouldn't put it past the feline to follow him.

"Achoo!" sneezed Sawyer.

"Blesh you again," said Finn.

The black Lab lowered his body to the ground and quietly barked into one of the cracks beneath the garage, in case it was the Echo he knew.

"Echo, it's me—Finn. The cardinal and blue jay told me—I forget when though—that Mean Mr. Caleb's carrots are just about ready for eatin'."

Finn didn't care for carrots, as noted earlier, though he knew some dogs, like Sawyer, who did. Regardless, he was more than happy to pass on the birds' information. Mean Mr. Caleb's yard was right behind Sawyer's Kingdom. Sawyer would probably get Finn to join him on a carrot raid; Finn would do anything for a friend.

Wait—he should have been miles away from the old neighborhood by now! Maybe he got turned around. His visit with the Vicar Pig had unsettled him. But he'd walked for so long since then… Was this a mirror world?

"Finn, my old pal!" cried Echo—it *was* the same Echo! "Jenny the cardinal and Agnes the blue jay are nice birds and good friends, nothing like those hawks that sometimes circle above or Archimedes the Owl who tries to snatch us up when it gets dark. He almost caught Mr. Whiskers last night."

Finn had never met Archimedes, but he'd heard the owl knew magic. The black Lab was going to whip out his only joke—that he'd always heard that Archimedes was a hoot, but he knew Echo lived in fear of the owl. Poor Mr. Whiskers (also known as Floppy in the warren)—he was the kind of bunny that inspired others to chase him, for food or sport, for he had one ear that stood straight up and one that flopped to the side; he was easy to spot, and nature abhors things and creatures that are abnormal.

Wait, wait—again all this seemed so familiar. How could he be so far away yet be in Sawyer's yard talking predatory birds with Echo? Finn had no idea—this Great Journey, his quest, was making his noggin spin—but he sure missed his own Kingdom. Who was guarding his backyard from Alley Cat now?

"We've already been at Mean Mr. Caleb's carrots but, alas, some from our warren got caught in his fencing," Echo said. "I freed Floppy just as Archimedes was descending. It was terrifying. I don't know why he bothers us and leaves Alley Cat and the Realists alone."

Finn became aware of a whole bunch of eyes blinking at him. They were like stars in the sky. After saying hi to each and every set of eyes (and swearing to himself that he'd never chase another bunny rabbit), he asked, "Who are the Realists?"

The younger rabbits giggled.

"You're on a quest, yes?" Echo asked. "A Great Journey? Word travels fast. Sad to say, we can't help you, but you'll meet the Realists soon enough, I'm sure of it."

Finn felt a moment of relief before realizing he still didn't know who or what the Realists were.

But when Sawyer started barking about the pirates again, the black Lab promptly forgot ever hearing the word "Realists." Finn bid his farewell to everyone in the warren—one at a time. But most of the younger ones had disappeared when Sawyer began barking.

"Pay attention to the pirates' booty, Finn," Echo said, his voice coming from beneath the garage. "The creamy Lab knows all."

And indeed, Sawyer, was a cream-colored Labrador retriever, except for three spots on his back. It would be easy to mistake him for an English white Lab, but the truth was that he was a yellow Lab, as Labrador retrievers only come in three colors: black, yellow, and chocolate, although there can be variations. Why Sawyer was creamy was a mystery (he was the only one in his litter to come out that color), but he was beautiful to look at it, a real handsome fellow. It looked like someone had drawn around his eyes with a thick black pencil, and his eyelashes were so white that from certain angles it looked like he didn't have any.

Now, Sawyer's three spots were...yellow! Sometimes it seemed like the yellow spots moved each time Finn saw his dear friend, but that was just in his head. Sawyer called it his treasure map, though no one knew why. If you stood behind him, you could see a yellow spot on his lower back (slightly off-centered) and one on his upper left side (the heart side). Both of these were light; if it was overcast, there was a possibility you might not notice them. The third one was on his right side (as seen from the back), almost equidistant from the other spots. It was the largest one, and the only one that looked really yellow. Sawyer was fond of saying that that would have been his color, if he wasn't special (or so Sawyer's Lad had told him). His best pal had also said to Finn that it was too bad he didn't have a spot on his tummy, for Sawyer was fond of belly rubs (Finn shared the same predilection), and he thought that a yellow spot might have made his tummy stand out.

When he first moved to the neighborhood, the cream-colored Lab used to say that yellow was the color he was supposed to be, because that was what the people in his First House had told him. They thought that Sawyer was a freak. His First House was a house of Hurters. They hit him and kicked him, even when he was a puppy. It was terrible. They even burned the inside of one of his ears with a cigarette. The Hurters made him sleep outside on a concrete porch without a roof, rain or shine. This was some place down South (which explained Sawyer's exotic accent). Then one day, he was sprung ("rescued" the Lad called it) and after a harrowing truck ride north (Sawyer hated car rides ever since; Finn loved them), he ended up in what the dogs' Big Uns called Mondauk County, Pennsylvania, "which is," Sawyer was fond of saying, "a really great place to live if you're a dog. It's filled with cookies, even if they are kept in a cupboard. So many cookies. But it would be so much nicer if I could serve myself." Now Sawyer told people that cream was the color he was supposed to be, just like fox red Labs are exactly the color they were meant to be, not just another mutation of yellow.

While Finn agreed with him about the plentiful cookies (his were kept on top of a scary-looking tall chrome robot named Fridge, who didn't talk as much as sigh at regular intervals), Finn bet that Sawyer wouldn't think Mondauk was so magical if he ate his Lad's shoes!

With his snout, Finn pushed his basketball to Sawyer who pushed it back in the same manner. It was a traditional greeting among retrievers, for the various breeds tended to retrieve only so they could retrieve again, so they really never *gave* in the traditional sense, thus giving was only done between friends (or retrievers who were fixing to be friends). Finn, who was very particular about his basketball and always a little worried about it, had nothing to fear with Sawyer, for besides being his best friend, Sawyer didn't retrieve. It had to do with his upbringing. Since he'd always been chained up on the concrete day and night, there was rarely a chance to run after something, and as far as bringing it back, well, the Hurters had no interest in their part of the fetch game. (Being chained up on the concrete may be why Sawyer's sniffer was so attuned: he'd had nothing else to do *but* sniff! He always knew what was cooking in each kitchen in the nearby houses, and he could sense a storm well before any other dog in the neighborhood—or at least he could in the one Finn recently left).

"Sawyer," Finn said, "before we go on this adventure with the, um, the…"

"Pirates," Sawyer said matter-of-factly. "You have to be brave to face—"

A drill went off in a nearby yard, and the creamy Lab dropped to the ground, crawled beneath Finn (as much as he could; mostly it was just his snout), and lay perfectly still, shivering. Finn could hear his friend's teeth chatter. Like Sawyer, Finn was afraid of Baron Thunder (better known as Mr. Boom), as well as fireworks, the scourge of summer, but Finn knew that Sawyer was terrified by *any* loud noises.

"It's just a Big Un tool," Finn said, "One that goes *whrrrr* for a little bit. It tends to start and stop, but I'm here, buddy-pal."

Sawyer removed his snout from under the black Lab. "You and me, Finn, womb to tomb."

They pressed their paws together, which was another traditional Lab greeting.

"Tell me what's bothering you," said the wise, fully composed cream-colored Lab, as he stretched. That seemed to be one of Sawyer's favorite activities besides sniffing and sneezing and creating adventures—stretching.

When Alley Cat came walking along the top of the tall wooden fence (similar to the one in Finn's backyard), both dogs immediately took notice. (Finn thought: he did follow me! But why?)

"Just passing through, boys," Alley Cat said. "Say, that's a nice basketball, Finn. Didn't know you played," he purred with a wink.

The orange-and-blue-striped basketball had rolled away since their traditional retriever greeting. Finn lunged for his basketball before Alley Cat could. He didn't know what the feline was up to, for he'd seen Finn play basketball many times before.

Alley Cat laughed. "As you were, boys," he said. Then he scurried across the fence top before jumping outside of the yard.

"Cats," Finn mumbled.

"How does a cat say goodbye?" Sawyer asked.

Finn truly didn't know.

" 'See ya litter!' "

The boys didn't have much time to yuk it up (Finn didn't find cat humor all that funny anyway), for a scrambling sound came from the far side of the yard.

Sawyer pointed towards the ramshackle garage again and raised his snout to sniff at the same time. "Pirates, I tell you. There's a foulness about the air." He turned to face his friend. "Then again, I just passed a little gas, so…"

But Finn thought he recognized the elusive scent of buccaneers too. (He was able to differentiate it from Sawyer's recent indiscretion.) The Boy had once read a book to him called *Treasure*

Island, and it was filled with pirates, and Finn used to imagine that they smelled like maggot cheese.

There was more scrambling, and from around the corner of the garage came Becky, the chocolate Labrador retriever. Now in the book, *The Adventures of Tom Sawyer*, it was Tom, not Huck, who was sweet on Becky, but in Mondauk County, Becky was Finn's girlfriend.

Finn was astounded that he'd found both Sawyer and Becky on his Great Journey. Is it possible that he'd circled back around and landed next door to his former home? No, no, he'd gone so far in his wanderings—hadn't he?

Becky bounded towards him, and they sniffed each other, their tails wagging so fast, you would have thought they'd just take off and fly through the air. Becky wore a turquoise neckerchief that made her look especially fetching to Finn. But Becky was more than just a pretty face; they called her the Sleeping Lion because, well, she slept more than any Lab they knew, but also because she could be particularly fierce when the situation called for it.

Sawyer stretched again then dropped and rolled around in the grass, while he watched his two friends reacquaint themselves.

"Where have you been?" Becky asked Finn. She was already lounging in the grass. (Becky was laid back and didn't let much startle her including the drill that broke the calm.) "I heard you ran away, looking for your roots or something like that, as if you were a plant instead of a Labby. We have toes and pads, not roots. You don't have to run away to see those—just look down."

Finn felt bashful around Becky. He liked the way her pinkish name tag caught the light, so he concentrated on that until he could get his bearings. "Well," he said, one of his paws absently digging in the dirt. "I'm looking for an answer. Two actually since I saw the Vicar. See, I ate the Boy's shoes, and now I'm on a Great—"

Sawyer's nose shot straight up, his nostrils going a mile a minute (two units of measurement that dogs generally disregarded).

"Squirrel!" cried Sawyer, and the three Labs were off chasing the eastern grey squirrel the others in his scurry called Mr. Nutball, an unfortunate name, but he was descended from a long line of Nutballs. His first name was actually Fred. (This was not the squirrel that had previously gone after the black Lab.) Mr. Nutball and Finn were acquainted through Echo, but Finn still chased him once in a while out of habit, though most of the time they shared the dog's backyard Kingdom peacefully. There was enough room.

(How did Mr. Nutball get here? Finn wondered. Echo and Jenny and Agnes too? Was the great wide Wold actually kinda small?)

Sawyer was right on Mr. Nutball's heels, and Becky was coming around from the other direction. Mr. Nutball winked at Finn and said, "Glad to see you came home," before ascending the nearest tree, then jumping and scampering partially down a sycamore in the next yard (which looked to Finn like the sycamore in his own yard).

The three Labs gathered around panting. Mr. Nutball scurried along a limb and (feeling safe) leapt back to a tree in the creamy Lab's yard (right over the dogs), then made an impressive jump to the fence between Sawyer and Becky's Kingdoms, but the Labs paid little attention. It looked like the Sleeping Lion was going to take a nap. (Becky made napping an art form.) To Finn, there was no dog more beautiful than Becky, none smarter, funnier, or more congenial. Her chocolate fur was so rich, and he loved the way she always wore a colorful neckerchief. Whether she was really Finn's girlfriend was open to conjecture, since they'd never been on more than a playdate, but Sawyer said they were the Royal Couple, and Sawyer was usually the last word on a great many matters, which is why Finn had hoped the creamy Lab would be able to answer his questions.

"AAAAAAH! FINN!" They could hear scurrying on the other side of the wooden fence, and Mr. Nutball launched himself from the top of it to the roof of the garage. His screams were followed by a THUD below.

"Go through the *hole*, Jim," Sawyer said like he'd said it a thousand times. "Jim thinks there are secret holes in the fence that are invisible until you try and go through them," Sawyer told Finn, as Becky gently snored. "He's always looking for things that aren't anywhere 'cept where they belong. Sometimes he doesn't see what's right in front of him." Perception problems, the cream-colored Lab said, and Finn nodded even though he wasn't sure what Sawyer meant. He was too busy being amazed that he'd somehow found all of his friends.

The creamy Lab sneezed, and the black Lab said, "Blesh you," feeling that bleshing was okay in this part of the Wold.

Mr. Nutball came whizzing by, but the dogs just watched. Before the squirrel caught the nearest branch and disappeared into the tree's drapery, Mr. Nutball doffed an imaginary cap to Finn and was gone by the time Jim came bounding through the hole in the fence that Becky had used, looking this way and that for the squirrel.

"Coulda sworn…" he mused. "Hmm…droppings."

Becky roused herself for the group hug. Jim was a golden retriever. His Big Uns lived a couple of houses over. Jim was always escaping; he was even better at escaping than Sawyer, and Sawyer once ran so far, he was spotted halfway across the county. Sawyer had mellowed (a little) since. But the golden retriever could not be held; Jim's Big Uns had tried everything, except tying him up, which they wouldn't do. It wasn't that he didn't love his Big Uns, and he adored his Lass, a wisp of a girl who loved to crash Lab meetings and spend her time hugging the dogs, petting them, and feeling their ears. (Well, they were *retriever* meetings, goldens being cousins to the noble Labradors and equally noble). His Lass always had pockets full of cookies, but even without the cookies, the retrievers loved her. It was hard not to. She always smelled like strawberries, and she thought everything the dogs did was funny, even the stuff that wasn't.

Sawyer filled Becky and Jim in on the pirates-in-the-garage situation, and they were up for an adventure. Sawyer could make dandelion sniffing seem exciting, but when it came to planning his adventures, the dogs knew he was rather meticulous.

"I think I see one," Jim cried, pointing, and the gang turned their heads, but Finn turned his noggin back around in time to see Jim eat a dandelion and try to quickly cover the evidence with dirt. Finn would eat one, but Sawyer might get upset; besides, there were buccaneers in the garage.

Finn blinked twice, as he watched two mice the color of charcoal (carrying tiny wardrobe bags) make their way to the back of the garage. So the Vicar Pig was right: there were black mice! Finn felt an instant affinity with them, even after he saw a tiny skull and crossbones flag being hoisted on top of the garage. (A sliver of a twig was used as the flagpole.)

"Don't we need weapons or a map?" Jim asked. (Jim could be very goofy, but he also quite practical.)

Sawyer bared his teeth: "We come with weapons, but good thieves don't need any weapons—and I'm the map."

Finn and the other dogs were as attentive as they could be, but no one seemed to understand the part about the map.

"We're thieves?" Jim asked. He seemed a bit alarmed. Finn was concerned too, but Sawyer always led them to safety. The worst that ever happened on one of Sawyer's adventures was that a bee stung Finn on his rump. Finn whispered (or tried to) in Jim's ear:

"It's make-believe." Finn wasn't sure that was true, and he hated fibbing to a good pal, but Jim was shaking just a little.

"My Lass, she wouldn't like me thieving," Jim whispered back (or tried to), but he was calmer now.

Sawyer stretched *and* sneezed. The cream-colored Lab winked, and Finn knew the adventure had begun. It must be said that dogs generally don't know how to wink, but they recognized each other's attempts.

How Sawyer knew that his spots were a map, not even he knew for sure. He'd told Finn long ago that the spots had to mean *something*. Since he was always the one planning the adventures, the other dogs took the creamy Lab at his word, although only Finn realized that they'd never used Sawyer as a map for any of their exploits before—and he promptly forgot about the idea, as did the other retrievers.

Becky, always the bravest (when she was awake that was) volunteered to go into the garage first. To go through the old, weather-beaten garage door, she had to squeeze her way in, but there were no other clear options. The door was warped enough that there were a couple of openings, but only one big enough for a dog to go through.

"Watch for splinters," Sawyer said.

"I don't know him," Becky said. "Splinters, I mean. Is he going to join—YEOW!"

"Splinters," Finn and Sawyer said, as they (carefully) followed her.

Jim went last. But he was afraid the splinters would get caught in his long coat and then attack him later when he was asleep under the porch (his favorite spot once they'd left Old Man Winter behind).

Jim (carefully) backed out of the door. "I'm going through the window…or something else," Jim said. While the garage did have windows on either side of the structure, they were high up, and the one on the left was close to the fence and would be extremely difficult to access. Finn and Sawyer exited the garage to watch.

"But how…?" Finn started to ask.

"Give him a minute," Sawyer said.

"Guys? Guys?" Becky stuck her snout out of the opening of the garage door, but not close enough to be attacked by splinters again. "It's, um, kinda spooky in here all by myself." Though she was brave, a creepy old garage could unsettle anyone.

Finn stuck his paw into the opening and placed it atop Becky's. "We'll be right there," he said.

"Jim might be there sooner," Sawyer added, smiling.

Jim fixed his fur, then backed up.

"Mind the dandelions please," Sawyer said. "I've counted most of them, and I'm about halfway through smelling them all."

There came a breeze and when Sawyer lifted his sniffer, Jim ate another dandelion. (Labs are not great at counting; Jenny and Agnes had once suggested to Finn it was because he didn't have any thumbs, and they'd witnessed various Big Uns counting on their fingers, and they always included their thumbs—which made about as much sense as anything else.)

Sawyer's nose was always on the lookout for the one dandelion that smelled significantly different from all others; at least that was the way Finn understood it. Maybe that was his best friend's quest. Whether this special dandelion actually existed, Finn didn't know. He was always worried for Sawyer that this one-of-a-kind dandelion grew in another dog's Kingdom, but the cream-colored Lab pooh-poohed the thought. Finn admired his best friend's belief in his belief.

While they waited for Jim to case the garage, looking for an opening that would be more kind to his longer hair, Sawyer drew close to Finn. "A Great Journey? I heard from Echo."

Finn's tail wagged. "Yes, yes, but I think I'm lost because it seems like I'm not terribly far away. I'm in your Kingdom; I'm in your yard. I don't understand."

"You're exactly where you're supposed to be," Sawyer said. "You're still on a Great Journey."

Sneeze.

"Blesh you."

Stretch.

"I have two questions," Finn said.

"We might only have time for one right now," Sawyer responded. "Is that okay? You can get lost again and come over tomorrow for the second one—unless the second one is about what happens when we *die*."

Finn nodded his head.

"Continue on your journey, Finn. There's one out there in our Wold who can answer your second question better than I can, I promise you, my friend. Some animals have more lives than others. But what's the first question?"

Finn asked, "Are my ears made of *SILK*?"

Sawyer chuckled (as much as a dog can chuckle) and said, "Are mine? We have different ears but the same kind."

Finn rubbed his face against Sawyer's ears and thought for a few seconds. "Well, they sure do feel soft, so does that mean they're made—"

From inside the garage: "Hurry it up, gents. It smells like feet in here—and not good feet, like my Little Lady's feet," Becky said, and Finn nodded. Becky had shared her Little Lady's feet with him once, which made the tiny girl giggle with delight.

"You'll find your answer," Sawyer said to his best friend. "Just remember to see…"

"I'm ready!" Jim barked. "I'm going in through the skylight!"

"…what's right in front of you."

After checking with an increasingly nervous Becky, Sawyer told Jim that there wasn't a skylight. Jim nodded. "Backup plan then," he said.

Beneath the garage window on the right was a pile of some upside down white plastic buckets. They were stacked like wayward stairs.

Jim took off and jumped upon the first bucket, then climbed up the next one. The one beneath the window was stacked higher than the one Jim was on, but he took a deep breath and jumped. The tub tottered a little, so Jim stood on his hind legs to balance himself, then drove his head into the side of the garage, which propelled him back to the grass (unhurt except for a mildly throbbing noggin).

Jim could have been in the circus, Finn thought, except for his perception problems.

"Could have sworn there was a window there," said Jim, unruffled.

"It's in the center," Sawyer pointed out. "Up there."

"I know," Jim said. "I just meant the *other* window. It was closer."

"The window that isn't there?" Sawyer asked, trying not to laugh. Labs love to laugh—at themselves, each other, even the weather (except when Mr. Boom made his presence known; Sawyer, in particular, had what you would call a difficult relationship with the Baron—he scared the Lab half to death).

Jim made for the tubs again.

Finn peeked through the garage door opening and gave Becky a play-by-play of the action thus far. He even mentioned that he was on a Great Journey, but she just said, "Aren't we all?"

Once the tallest of the stack of tubs stopped wobbling, Jim reached out with one free paw, pushed the window open (which made a screeching sound that reminded Finn of cats), jumped with his front paws lightly touching the window frame, and landed with a clang on something that made other things clang.

"Jim? Jim?" Becky cried. "Where are you? Do you still have all your pieces?"

"My head is in a birdcage," Jim responded. "Other than that…"

Finn said to Becky through the opening: "Maybe you should be out here and be the lookout. If Sawyer's right about these pirates, there could be more coming."

Becky laughed. "Stop trying to be so protective. Besides, I'd probably just end up taking a nap. This is my adventure too." The matter was closed.

Finn and Sawyer squeezed into the garage and indeed: Jim's head was lodged in an enormous birdcage.

Sawyer laughed and said, "I guess they adopted this golden retriever from an aviary!"

That was the thing (besides being of the same or related breed) that Finn had in common with his friends: they were all adopted, and they'd all had a rough time of it before now, before life was good. That was what Finn left behind when he stepped into the wide Wold: a life of pillows, cookies, belly rubs, and snuggling.

"That must have been one big bird," Finn said, as they dislodged Jim's head from the cage. "Did you know it?" Finn asked Sawyer, for the black Lab knew his pal was quite friendly with a number of birds besides Jenny and Agnes.

Jim shook the dust off his fur. "Guess they just traded up!" His nose twitched.

Sneeze!

"Blesh—"

Becky and Sawyer sneezed too, one after the other. The garage was dusty (not just Jim), and it seemed as if the golden retriever had just woken the decrepit structure with his exertions.

As soon as the dust had settled (and bleshings exchanged), the Sniffer had his snout in the air again. Finn knew that Sawyer's nose could differentiate between mouse droppings and the sweat of a group of pirates, but Finn figured if the pirates were still in the garage they would have attacked the dogs already.

All of their tummies were rumbling.

"We should have brought provisions," Becky said with an eye on the garage door in case there was a frontal attack

Jim reached into his pocket for the dandelions he'd stashed there, but dogs don't have pockets, a fact that Jim had forgotten (again) in his haste to harvest a few of the weeds. Finn thought that a good thing; Sawyer might get upset, though it took a lot for the creamy Lab to get into a bad mood. Sawyer was an especially upbeat pooch.

Finn had been sure to bring his orange-and-blue-striped basketball with him into the garage. (You could never turn your back on Alley Cat, he believed.) At first he thought it might be a bad idea. Who knew? Maybe pirates liked to play basketball. (He made a mental note to inspect any future laundry baskets for pirates, just in case he ever completed his Great Journey and discovered the answers he so desired.) But in the end, he felt comforted having the basketball with him; it was a little bit of home in the wild—and he missed home, even if the Big Uns and the Boy didn't miss him. (He stifled a sob.) He imagined the Big Uns buying the Boy a new pair of shoes, and he knew the Boy would have asked Finn if he thought they were sharp or not. Finn never knew what that meant, but the Boy had always been happy with whatever response he gave.

Finn had been thinking so hard on these things, he hadn't realized he'd been barking out loud. Becky licked his nose, and the boys gathered around him. A bouncing sound interrupted the group hug.

Up and down, up and down, up and down.

Finn picked up his basketball with his mouth. Nope, it wasn't his ball that was bouncing. No one was dribbling it.

"I know a Chesapeake Bay retriever who lives in the house behind Mean Mr. Caleb's," Jim said. "His name is Harper, but everyone calls him Joe. Big pooch. Could help us out."

Up and down, up and down, up and down.

"But then we'd be down one dog while you left to get him—and what if he wasn't allowed out to play?" Sawyer said. "Joe might have to make a break for it, and there's no telling if the Chessie would want to tussle with pirates over the treasure."

"Treasure?" the other dogs said in unison.

"But we're going to have to fight pirates for it?"

Sawyer rummaged a bit in a corner and came back with a bunch of black bandit masks that he must have stashed in the garage for just this moment. (They were actually old Halloween masks meant for little kids.)

"Well, we're thieves, aren't we?"

"Thieves—really?" cried Becky.

"Sorta. But it shouldn't come to an out-and-out fight if we can be sneaky—or if they're clumsy." He handed out the bandit masks, but none of the dogs seem to know how to put them on, though they helped one another. (The lack of opposable thumbs was blamed.) Sawyer obviously had practiced, for he looked positively dashing. No one could tell if Finn's mask was on right or not, since the black of the mask blended in with the rich color of his fur. Becky wore hers like another neckerchief. Jim wore his like a hat.

"Just follow my lead," Sawyer said. "I learned my part from my previous excursions, and I know it well."

There was a crash behind a table that was on its side. The retrievers backed into one another. A sunbeam found its way through the cracks and illuminated the banana seat on one of the retired bicycles.

"Pirates!" cried Becky and Jim.

"Mice pirates!" barked Finn.

And indeed, on the banana seat were the two mice Finn had seen earlier, only now they were dressed like pirates, with real buccaneer gear (but tiny): scuffed black boots (the mice were tottering on two legs as they jumped *up and down, up and down, up and down*), wide belts with scabbards, a big golden hoop earring in one ear, and red headscarves that peaked out beneath their black pirate hats, which were adorned with the skull and crossbones. One mouse had a pretend hook for a hand; the other had a black eye patch that was so big it covered most of his face; only part of one blinking eye could be seen. They both had tiny cutlasses, which they rattled in a menacing manner; one of them held his with his tail. They jumped from the banana seat to a bouncy circle and, well, bounced until they landed on the metal edge that encircled the old trampoline. Maybe this was the treasure, Finn thought, eyeing the bouncy circle, for the pirates seemed quick to defend it.

In his free hand, the mouse with the eye patch had a spyglass, but when he brought it up to his eye, it appeared to make him dizzy, and his friend steadied him with his hook hand, which made the eye patch mouse go, "Ooomph!" for the hook, though pretend, was pointy. The jab also pushed Eye Patch (for lack of a better name) back off balance, and he reached for his friend's hook to right himself, but the Hook Mouse's hook, being fake, POPPED off his wee hand, and Eye Patch tumbled forwards off the metal circle, taking the now hookless mouse with him., and they bounced back the way they came.

The dogs had all crowded around one another, first out of fear. No one besides Sawyer had ever seen a pirate before (and Sawyer was known to spin tales to get an adventure off the ground). But they remained huddled together, rather than run off, because the show was so entertaining—and because the pirates were mice, though even mice armed with tiny swords were dangerous.

Without warning a cloud of dust hovered above the banana seat, and when it settled, the two mice stood there clasping paws and taking bows while the dogs barked in approval. They mice started jumping *up and down*, but Eye Patch slipped in the dust and backwards he went. The other mouse (who had his hook again) grinned in a sheepish manner and jumped after his friend, and that was the last the retrievers saw of the pirates for a while (but not of the mice).

Finn heard Alley Cat snickering outside the garage, and he put a paw on his basketball. Was Alley Cat laughing because he was entertained by the mice or was he laughing because he planned to eat the tiny pirates? Finn was pretty sure cats ate mice. Dogs did not, as far as he knew, though his tummy rumbled at the thought of a meal or even a cookie. The wide Wold didn't seem to have any cookies available. Maybe Sawyer would lend him one.

More disturbing was what Sawyer had said about Finn living just next door. While it was true that they were neighbors, Finn again asked himself: had he traveled far and wide only to find himself back where he started? Was that even possible? Maybe everyone had moved to this part of the Wold, except Mr. Turtle, who he'd gone looking for after his contentious chat with the Vicar Pig.

"Okay, gang," Sawyer said. "The pirates have taken themselves out of the adventure, so all that's left is for us to steal their booty (so to speak)."

Finn gently nudged Becky who'd fallen asleep.

The chocolate Lab stretched. Sawyer and Becky were big stretchers. Finn once saw Sawyer put his front paws on the floor and stretch while his hind legs were still on a bed. Finn had tried it at home and fell into a tumble at the Boy's feet. The Boy giggled until he fell in his own heap next to Finn. *Sigh.* That was a good giggle day. Why oh why did he have to munch on the Boy's shoes?

"Another pirate!" cried Jim. He was in the classic pointing pose with one leg raised. Becky cried, "Stand back!" as she tackled a dressing dummy. Finn ran to his girlfriend (avoiding the broken toys and gardening tools that littered the floor) in case there were more enemies around.

"I don't think this is a pirate," Becky said, as she licked the dressing dummy. "Not unless it's a really big dusty pirate."

Jim went to inspect, being careful not to get too close. "We just saw tiny pirates, so why couldn't there be big ones?" Jim asked. Finn and Sawyer exchanged a look. Jim stepped on a rake. Finn grabbed the handle between his jaws before it could rap Jim's schnozz. Becky continued to lick the dressing dummy. Finn thought their treasure hunting party was falling apart until he saw Sawyer's snout raised.

"The Sniffer!" Finn cried, and all the dogs crowded around the cream-colored Lab.

"What is it?" Finn whispered (or tried to).

"Did you eat two of my dandelions?" Sawyer asked Jim.

"You can smell that he ate them?" Becky asked, as Jim hung his head.

"No, he has a few petals on his chin."

Jim's tongue shot out to erase the evidence, but it was too late. "I'm sorry." Sawyer winked at his friend to let him know it was okay, but it looked more like a special blink; only canines and human children know the difference. To human adults and other animals it would look Sawyer had something in his eyes or possibly was signaling SOS, which would be odd, as there has never been a dog that owned a boat. But children learned how to wink from their dogs, only no one knows what they're doing; it looks like they're just blinking at one another. Labs find this funny and will roll around with the children, laughing at the whole idea of dogs and kids trying to blink SOS.

Sawyer's snout shot straight up in the air again.

Becky, now wide awake, pointed and barked, "The Sniffer!"

"What do you smell?" Finn asked Sawyer.

"Pirates...or cats?" asked Jim, as a tremor went down his body. He started to cry but Finn nuzzled him until he stopped.

"Chicken," Sawyer said. "Fried. Homemade. Mrs. Beckett from over on Highland Avenue."

"That's four blocks away!" cried Becky.

"She makes the best pies," said Jim who'd always make several attempts to snatch one that was cooling on the Becketts' kitchen windowsill during his escapes. He was frequently caught as he always saw ways to reach the windowsill that just weren't there. Jenny and Agnes often stole the pie and shared it with the golden retriever.

"Fried chicken," Becky said, as she rolled on her back but only briefly as there was no one present who could rub her tummy *or* feed her fried chicken.

Sawyer looked to his best friend and said, "Ready, Freddie?"

This led to an intense discussion, since Finn and Becky and Jim didn't know a Freddie and wondered if Sawyer was having a fit. Finn said his name, his full name, very slowly to Sawyer.

"Does Freddie look like me?" Finn asked, a tad anxious. To think that there was another Lab walking around with his face was disturbing.

"I knew an Eddie...or maybe it was an Ernie," said Becky between yawns. "He was a cocker spaniel though."

"He's a nice kid," Jim said. "Lives two yards down from my Kingdom."

"Oh, I know him," Finn said. "It's Ernie though, not Freddie...or Eddie. Hangs around with the blonde spaniel, Woofer."

"Woofer lives next door to Joe," Jim said. "Smart pooch, that one. One time he designed an escape plan for me—not that I needed the help, but..."

Sawyer covered his snout with his paws and sighed audibly.

Finn was once again confused. How could he have put such distance between himself and the Vicar Pig, only to end up in his old neighborhood? He wondered if the squirrels and rabbits had overtaken his backyard Kingdom. What if Alley Cat had moved in? Cats were notorious squatters.

"But if Ernie's not Freddie," Becky said, "then who is?"

"No, Ernie's Ernie," Jim said, "and Woofer is—"

Sawyer growled and everyone stopped talking.

"Forget Freddie," he said. "It's time we liberate the treasure before the pirates return—and they will come back."

"The mice pirates or the little dusty ones?" asked Becky, no longer struggling with the yawns.

Sawyer shook his head. "They're one and the same. Pirates…just pirates."

Finn could see his friend getting upset. He knew that Sawyer designed these adventures for maximum fun, even if they were sometimes a little scary like this one with the pirates.

"What we need to find first is a map," Finn said. He wondered why Sawyer would lead them into the garage without one—a real one—but as usual, the cream-colored Lab had it all figured out.

"I told you already: *I'm* the map," Sawyer said (slightly exasperated), and the other dogs remembered and went, "Oooh!" They knew immediately that Sawyer was referring to his yellow spots. For years, when various pooches asked "why?" or even "what are they for?" in regards to the spots, Sawyer always answered that someday they would lead to something great. The creamy Lab had told the black Lab that he knew he was so marked because the spots meant *something*, and if they meant *something*, then it must mean something great, because, generally, Labs are upbeat creatures, their feelings regarding fireworks, cars backfiring, doors slamming, Baron Thunder, and, of course, cats notwithstanding.

The dogs ditched their masks and surrounded Sawyer, studying his spots.

None of the dogs could make heads or tails of what they meant. Finally, Finn asked his friend, "Will you show us?" But before Sawyer could, Jim jumped in.

"What's the treasure?" the golden retriever asked, salivating a little. "Cookies?" Everyone except Sawyer barked at hearing the word "cookies." There are very few things as important to dogs as cookies. Finn, though a stranger in this mirror version of the Wold, knew that when eating a cookie, dogs are transformed, briefly, into their best selves. They may be grabby or pushy when it came to attaining a cookie, but once it began to reach their bellies, dogs experienced what was called "a slice of heaven" by the Big Uns. Though Finn could never have put it that way, he and Becky and Jim were drooling, looking forward to the crunchy slices of heaven. (Becky even drooled cute, Finn thought, momentarily distracted from thoughts of cookies-to-come.)

Sawyer sighed again. "Focus, lady and gents, for behold, we are on the threshold of a treasure so great that only Huckleberry here can know its true worth, for he alone knows the question to ask and only he could *possibly* be able to show us that 'all that glitters is not gold.' " (Sawyer paid attention when the Big Uns read to his Lad.)

While Becky and Jim mourned the lack of a cookie-orientated treasure, Finn leaned into Sawyer and said, "Tommy, before we find the treasure, I really should ask you my second question."

Sawyer licked his friend's nose. "You want to know about the *D* word and where we go afterwards, is that it?"

Finn nodded furiously. Becky and Jim asked him if he was broken.

Sawyer said, "We don't worry ourselves with the *D* word, my best of friends. Canines, we don't concern ourselves with such *d*epressive subjects. We retrieve. We chase. We sniff. We cuddle. We're the clown princes of the dog world; we bring joy, not *D* words."

Becky listened intently, while Jim licked his toes (but he was paying attention).

"To us, Finn," Sawyer said as he paced, "there is no end, just as there was no beginning: suddenly we were puppies, and who among us remembers retrieving their first ball? Now, we all had bad runs of it before we were rescued, but now we are where we belong—that includes you, Finn—and we are what we're made of— the soft and the tough. It's just hard to see sometimes."

"But the shoes…I chewed 'em. Now all I have is my basketball and my two ears, if they're worth anything.

"Is this really your Kingdom, Tommy? Is this the Wold I left?"

Sawyer attempted a shrug. "Who really knows? I feel real. Maybe you're home and maybe you're a million miles away, and we're just the vestiges of a dream."

That this could be a dream was something he'd thought before when he'd encountered King Mite, but hearing Sawyer say it sent shivers down his black fur. If this was a trace of a dream, the heartache felt heavier than anything he'd ever experienced.

"The important thing," Sawyer said, "is that we have everything we need to help Finn use the treasure, once we take possession of it."

"How are we supposed to read the map if you keep pacing?" Jim said to Sawyer, while Becky nuzzled Finn.

"I think what Sawyer was trying to say," Becky whispered to Finn (or tried to), "is that it's best if you lay the *D* word aside. It's not our word. It's not a Lab word."

"You know the *D* word too?" Finn whispered back (or tried to) while nervously rolling his orange-and-blue-striped basketball.

Here it must be noted (again) that Labs can't whisper. Most dogs can't, though the curly-tailed basenji can yodel; however they also sneeze a lot, more than Sawyer even. (Finn thought his best friend's sneeziness had to do with smelling all those dandelions.) Greyhounds have notoriously been known to play whisper-down-the-lane, minus the whispering, which made for a terrible game that the hounds always thought they'd get right the next time they played, but greyhounds have a distinctive bark that's more like a (soft) howl, developed during the days when they used to race for a bunch of screaming Big Uns, thus they didn't do subtle very well. In fact, keeping a secret was an impossibility for greyhounds, so there was always drama between them, even once they were rescued.

Jim thought he saw one of the theatrical mice and chased it until he collided with a silver serving tray propped up against an Easy-Bake Oven. As he backed up, an old bicycle pump attacked him. By the time he realized that the black mouse he was chasing was just a reflection of his own shiny black schnozz in the serving tray, the bicycle pump had him pinned. Finn picked up his basketball with his teeth lest it get caught up in Jim's misadventure.

A yawning Becky pushed the pump off her golden friend, who went from shuddering to scrambling.

"Thank you," said Jim, as he brushed himself off and tried to look nonchalant, which is a fancy way of saying that Jim tried to appear unconcerned that he'd been bested by a tarnished serving tray, a child's toy oven, and a bicycle pump that had seen better days.

"Zzzzzzz," was Becky's response; she could fall asleep at the drop of a hat.

"The map!" cried Jim, who'd seen the creamy Lab pacing in the serving tray and had an idea. "We have to *turn* Sawyer to get it right! We need to…" He struggled for the next word; it was Big Un word he'd overheard when his house was being redecorated. "We need to *orient* Sawyer." He was barking so loud that Sawyer shushed him—no need to bring the Big Uns to the garage—but Jim was right: they needed to orient the creamy Lab. "Orient" was not a particularly canine word, certainly one Finn had never used before, but though the dogs all imagined different meanings or phrases, Finn thought of the word which he'd heard the boy read from Merriam the dictionary. According to the beast of a book, "orient" meant (and here Finn *really* relied on his Smart Bump) "to ascertain the bearings" of something (in this case, Sawyer), "bearings" meaning "a determination of position." Finn remembered a great many words from the Boy and Merriam, most of which he never heard again.

The black Lab informed the other dogs what he recalled and told them that Jim was right: they had to *move* Sawyer; they had to *orient* him.

Once the gang realized they were on the same page, they roused Becky who suggested that perhaps Sawyer's tail was like the needle on a compass. None of the other dogs were familiar with a compass, but Becky's Little Lady was a Girl Scout Brownie. Regardless, what Becky thought was that instead of pointing true north, Sawyer's tail pointed towards the treasure, which all the retrievers thought made about as much sense as anything else. The odd thing was that at the moment Sawyer's curled tail was pointing towards Finn and beyond him to what Sawyer had referred to as the bouncy circle, which Finn already thought was the treasure (but he'd held his tongue; he didn't want to spoil Becky's fun). But then the cream-colored Lab's tail relaxed and brushed the floor, and the dogs thought the compass concept might be a bust, and they went back to the idea of orienting Sawyer.

From behind a collapsed card table and some wounded beach chairs, they heard the tittering of mice. Finn swore he heard Alley Cat sniggering too, which made little sense to Finn, since he always thought that cats and mice were mortal enemies. Becky leaned into her boyfriend and told him to ignore them, but he still hugged his basketball.

They turned Sawyer around and around—and around once more until he was dizzy—but were no closer to figuring out the map or finding the treasure.

When the mice sneezed—for mice liked to sneeze in tandem, everyone in Sawyer's gang barked, "BLESH YOU!" The mice scampered away in fear, though that was clearly not the intention of the frustrated dogs.

Jim sat his rump on a Big Wheel seat.

"My Lass, she always asks me, 'Are you being silly?' and I always bark back, 'No, I'm being *Jim!*' and I'm sad until she gives me a cookie."

"Sawyer's not being silly, Jim," Becky said. "He's just dizzy."

"I'll say," Sawyer said.

"What kind?" Finn asked, for he was hungry.

"How many different kinds of dizzy are there?" Sawyer said to his best friend.

"No, I meant what kind of cookie does Jim's Lass give him when she gets his name wrong?"

"The crunchy kind," Jim answered, "of course.

"My Little Lady sometimes takes my noggin in her wee hands after I have a cookie and stares into my eyes," Becky said. " 'I'm looking into your soul,' she always says when she does this, and I always bark back (in a nice way) that I hadn't had time to straighten up or anything." Becky always thought she was guilty of something— an aftereffect of her abusive upbringing prior to her rescue and adoption. After telling the dogs her Little Lady story, she immediately fell asleep.

Finn asked, "What's a soul?" He thought it sounded like it could involve his *D* word question. "And how could Becky's soul— wake up, dear—need straightening up?" He thought of another word from the beast of a book: "disarray." Was that a bad *D* word too?

Jim tried to shrug and said, "I don't know really. I just tend to leave a mess."

"You leave some crumbs behind?" a fully awake and incredulous Becky asked.

"Not crumbs! Just drool," Jim cried before falling off the side of the Big Wheel, just missing a pair of expired tiki torches, as well as Mr. and Mrs. Pillar.

"Excuse you!" said Mr. Caterpillar.

"Dogs in a garage! Have you ever, Harold?" asked Mrs. Caterpillar.

"Never!" said Mr. Caterpillar, as the couple inched away. He turned his head and said, "Retrievers retrieve—they don't drive the Wheels, Big or otherwise."

"The chrysalis stage cannot come soon enough," Mrs. Caterpillar said. "This neighborhood is going to the dogs!"

"Retrievers retrieve!" Mr. Caterpillar shouted, as he and his wife shimmied up a slim branch that had poked through the left window.

While Finn and Sawyer discussed the map situation in earnest (Finn kept his bouncy circle treasure thought to himself, in case he was being silly like Jim), they couldn't help but overhear the Caterpillar couple, and Sawyer was ashamed. *Retrievers retrieve.* It was well known that Sawyer didn't retrieve. Finn leaned on his oldest friend. Sawyer had had a bad life before being rescued and adopted. Because of all the beatings and other tortures he endured from the Hurters down South, he never learned to access one of his most innate behaviors, only those he needed to survive (like eating); he never even knew what retrieving was until he saw a little boy and his German shepherd. Sawyer was chained up, and the chain didn't allow him to move off the slab of concrete where he spent all of his time. But as Sawyer watched the boy throw the ball and the shepherd bring it back, something inside of him yearned but he didn't what for. The shepherd (whose name was Rufus, but other dogs called him Fred because he looked like a Fred) was deliriously happy and seemed to be good at the job or the game or whatever it was. By the time Sawyer was rescued, he was too old to learn new tricks. Whenever his Lad threw the ball, Sawyer enjoyed watching its trajectory, but felt absolutely no need to chase after it and bring it back; it never even occurred to him.

Finn knew all of this because Sawyer was his best pal in the whole Wold. "Some Labs were made to *think* rather than *retrieve*," Finn said. "I mean, yes, we all think, but most of us spend bunches of time chasing after things, retrieving them. You don't retrieve 'cause you *think*, Tommy." Finn gestured with his nose. "This whole pirate adventure is happening only because you thought it up instead of running after tennis balls."

"Are they the fuzzy ones?"

"Yes, they tickle the tongue," Finn said. "So how about we find the treasure?" He was feeling a tad anxious. There was a heaviness in his Little White Tie.

"*Your* treasure," Sawyer said quietly.

Finn nodded although he didn't know what in the Wold his friend was talking about. *His* treasure?

It must be said that most dogs are very intelligent animals, although they are not very Woldly, so sometimes with other creatures, some dogs, like Finn, can seem very naïve. But with other dogs, they are intuitive, savvy at times, and, of course, goofy. Finn may not have known what Sawyer was talking about, but he knew finding this treasure (whether it was the bouncy circle or something else) was important to his friend, who seemed to be indicating that it would be important to Finn.

Mr. and Mrs. Caterpillar watched the Labs and the golden from the safety of their branch.

"Tsk, tsk," said Mrs. Caterpillar.

"The dog days of summer indeed," sniffed Mr. Caterpillar.

"It's fall, dear," his wife said.

"And fall they shall!" declared her husband.

Finn looked over the gang. Jim looked too pooped to pop, and Becky was curled up in a chocolate ball, soft little snores coming from the middle. He could have sworn she was awake a moment ago...

"C'mon, guys and gal!" Finn said. "We're not gonna find this treasure unless we mix our Smart Bumps with Becky's bravery and Sawyer's map and Jim's go-get 'em attitude."

Becky jumped out, which made the other dogs back up into a toy box, knocking it over. "It's just me, guys. I was resting my eyeballs." A jack-in-the-box went off, and all four dogs crowded together. Finn had his basketball in his mouth.

"I know those things," Becky said eventually, pushing it with her nose.

"Watch out, Becky," Jim said. "Next thing you know, Alley Cat'll being jumping out of the box."

Finn dropped his basketball and went to Becky's side. If anything happened to her...well, he didn't want to think about it. (He still didn't know how Becky and the boys were here, but it sure felt real. Still, he'd come so far, he thought, hadn't he?)

"My Little Lady had a one of these jack-in-the-box toys. Scared the cookies out of me at first," and all the other dogs shook their heads; being without one's cookies was too terrible to think about. "She would just turn that crank sticking out of the side, and the scary clown would jump out after this creepy music played."

Jim tried to snap his toes. He tried again. Nothing. "Wait, wait," he said. Still nothing. Finn could see the golden had clean forgotten that dogs can't snap.

"You have an idea…" Finn prompted.

"Well, Becky said we had to orient the Lab, but what if we're only looking at Sawyer's map as if it was…something…" Jim looked dejected. "I had it right at the tips of my toes."

But Sawyer picked up on what Jim was trying to say. "Maybe we've been looking at my map as if it were just a map of the ground. Look up."

The dogs did and it was like there was another garage floor (though not nearly as messy) on the walls. One area had a pegboard with rusty hammers and such hanging from it. Against another wall was a collection of snow shovels and dirt shovels and rakes covered in spider webs. There was even a spot where the rake that almost rapped Jim on the nose used to be. The back wall had an impressive array of old, big paintings in frames, most of them rusted; some of the rust had run down into the eyes of the people in the paintings or across landscapes or seascapes. (Finn knew those words from the Boy's homework, and just then, there was a twinge in his heart, for he feared he would never see the Boy or the Big Uns again. His eyes filled up, and Becky came over to nuzzle him, which made Finn feel a lot better, but the specter of wandering the Wold alone, never finding out the answers to his questions—no more cookies, no more belly rubs, no more Boy—scared him to his core.)

"Look in the corner," Sawyer said, and the dogs followed his gaze.

In the corners of the garage there were hung various bric-a-brac, to use a Big Un word, but in one corner was a round mirror that had suffered some water damage. It was hung about the height of the windows and was angled so it faced the window on the right.

Sawyer had his nose in the air again. Finn could see that Jim was worried about the dandelions he'd pulled up. (He'd already been forgiven for the ones he ate.)

"The Sniffer!" Finn and Becky cried. Jim was busy checking his tummy for dandelion evidence, for that was where, Finn knew, Jim thought he had a pocket like a 'Roo. The Boy had showed him one in a book once. The 'Roo bounced up and down and had a pouch on its belly.

"Just like a 'Roo, Finn...I think you've got the right idea," said Sawyer. The black Lab was astonished and embarrassed: had he been talking aloud or could Sawyer read his thoughts? "You talk out loud sometimes, at least when the basketball isn't in your mouth," his best friend said with a smile.

Sawyer didn't have his snout in the air to smell something; he was looking up at the old round mirror. Occasionally, he sized up the window that Jim had come through.

"Have the pirates returned?" Jim asked, and no one answered. Finn and Becky weren't being rude; they were following Sawyer's gaze. Eventually the creamy Lab lowered his noggin, looking intensely all around. Finally he pointed with his leg to something on the left side of the garage: the trampoline—what the dogs called the bouncy circle. It turned out that Becky's idea of Sawyer's tail being like the needle of a compass was right (at least when it was raised, the end facing the noggin), but instead of pointing towards a treasure, it had pointed towards the bouncy circle—unless that *was* the treasure, as Finn had thought. Becky was quite pleased with herself, even if she didn't know the significance of the bouncy circle.

As Sawyer suggested, the dogs cleaned the trampoline as best they could. (Labs and goldens weren't big cleaners.) Bouncy circles were generally foreign to them, though Sawyer said he remembered when it was a fixture in his yard, his Kingdom.

"You bounce on it," Sawyer said, "hence its name." The retrievers looked wary, but Becky said, "I'm game!" Sawyer put one of his paws over one of hers. "It's for Finn."

Finn was concerned. He'd never heard of a Lab bouncing on anything, let alone a round circle (still) decorated with dead leaves.

"Why?" the black Lab asked the creamy Lab, and Sawyer winked (blinked) at Becky, who was about to nap.

"Orient the Lab!" cried Becky, and she turned Sawyer this way and that. Jim jumped in to help and tried to steer the cream-colored Lab by his tail.

"Ow!"

"Sorry, buddy," Jim said. "No using the tail. Got it."

Finn sat on the dirty floor of the garage. His eyes were on Sawyer's yellow spots, and he tried to make sense of the map, as the dogs spun Sawyer round and round.

"I see it!" Finn barked, and he stopped Becky and Jim from continuing to turn around a slightly nauseous Sawyer, so that the creamy Lab was facing the garage door; they were behind him. "See: the biggest spot on his back?" Finn asked.

"The one on the right from our...?" Becky asked.

"Perspective," Sawyer suggested. His Lad had a Merriam too.

"Well, that big spot," Finn said, "it...it...*represents* us," Finn said (digging deep into his vocabulary), "or maybe it represents Sawyer; I guess I'm not sure. But look up at the mirror, then look at the open window. They're sorta the same shape as Sawyer's other two spots (but bigger, of course), and they're spaced apart about the same, if you get my drift." (The phrase "if you get my drift" he'd learned from the Boy, and it hurt his heart to use it.) The other dogs saw it too: the small yellow spot on Sawyer's back (which wasn't centered; it was more to the right) and the almost equally small spot on his upper left side were diagonal from each other like the round mirror in the back corner of the garage was diagonal from the window Jim had tumbled through.

"But what does it mean," Jim asked, as Becky growled at the former pirate mice who were sitting atop the Easy-Bake Oven sharing a piece of very stale-looking popcorn and watching the dogs. The mice took off at once, but one returned to retrieve the popcorn.

"I think the bigger spot is the bouncy circle," Sawyer said, although he'd never seen his own spots, not really. The Lad had tried to show him using two mirrors, so he had an idea; it wasn't an entirely successful endeavor. But Sawyer now knew how mirrors worked.

Becky lit up. "I know what the bouncy circle is for: to see into the mirror," she barked.

Sawyer placed himself in Becky's way, for she was about to leap upon the trampoline. "Like I said: it's for Finn...or it is for now."

Finn eyed the bouncy circle with suspicion. If this was the treasure, he was starting to think he would have been better off if they'd never found it!

"What if it wakes up and bounces me across town. I'm lost as it is…and Labs don't bounce. I don't think any dogs do—not this way."

"It can't wake up because it's not alive like us," Sawyer explained. "But I do agree with you: dogs don't usually bounce—except for you. You bounce. Just you—for now. The pirates have been vanquished (for the time being). I think the treasure is yours, and the key is in the round mirror."

"Aw!" cried Becky and Jim, but they nuzzled Finn anyway, and he knew that they were happy for him, even if he wasn't particularly happy himself.

"And what are…mirrors?" Finn asked.

Becky seemed to know. "My Lass plays with her mom's—Mrs. Big Un's—makeup sometimes, and she uses a mirror."

"But what are they *for*?" Finn wasn't playing with makeup.

"To look into," Sawyer answered, and he told the black Lab about his own introduction to mirrors. "It's like when you can see your reflection in your water bowl."

Finn had noticed his reflection but had always ignored it, not knowing what it was. "Oh," he said, wondering if the bouncy circle and the mirror were part of his Great Journey.

"Back up so you can get a running start," his best friend said between sneezes and bleshings. "I think you'll bounce right away. Just try to, well, stay in the center and bounce higher until you can see in the mirror."

Finn was dubious. The mirror was, for whatever reason, pretty high.

"He who hesitates," Sawyer said, "misses the cookie."

"There are cookies?" Jim asked.

"No one said anything about there being cookies," Becky said, trying to hide her drool.

"Bounce, Finn, bounce," Jim said, who proceeded to demonstrate by jumping into a dusty baby pool.

"I don't think—" Sawyer began.

"I hurt my rump," Jim reported from inside the wading pool. "I thought maybe every circle in here was bouncy."

"Clearly that's not true," Becky said as she helped Jim out of the pool. "It would have hurt less if it had water in it, I bet."

"I bet is right," Jim responded.

"Don't think about it too much, Finn," Sawyer said. "This is important: you want to bounce on your butt. Use your back legs to give you some height, but bounce on your rear end."

Finn thought he'd come too far to chicken out now. He'd survived the Vicar Pig's nastiness. Surely he'd survive a bounce or two—on his rump. He pawed the floor of the garage to mentally rev himself up, when without warning the pirate mice scurried into the scene, standing on a dilapidated end table that was missing a leg. They must have gotten dressed in a hurry, for one of them had a pirate hat on top of his pirate hat. The other fumbled with a buccaneer's pistol and ripe piece of cheese, so that he ended up turning and pointing the cheese up at the dogs in a threatening manner. With a combination of delicacy (so he wouldn't hurt the pirate mouse's little paw) and urgency (for he was famished), Jim woofed down the cheese. The mice pirates rattled their sabers, before turning and *jumping* upon the trampoline. The mice giggled, which was quite unbecoming for a pair of pirates. After their final bounce on the bouncy circle, they became a blur from which they emerged as they went flying across the garage. All that was left of their presence was a boot that was pierced through by a plastic hook and some distant giggling.

So Finn did as Sawyer had suggested (and the pirate mice had demonstrated), and before he knew it, he BOUNCED on his butt!

And UP went Finn and down and UP, his ears flapping, his eyes wide. Finn most decidedly did not like bouncing (the position—legs and tail outstretched so that his rear end was his center of gravity—was foreign to him), yet UP he went, then down and UP again.

"Um, Tommy, sometimes when I bounce, I get all turned around." Finn thought it was worth mentioning, for indeed, at the moment, he was facing away from the mirror.

Sawyer laughed. "You'll come around again soon enough...like right...now."

The black Lab felt a little motion sickness. "Isn't there an easier way?"

"Just keep your eyes closed whenever you start to turn around. It'll help, my friend, until you're used to it."

Finn took Sawyer at his word, and it seemed to ease his tummy (which had been rumbling anyway because he was sure he'd missed dinner).

"Now keep bouncing higher and higher," Sawyer said, but Finn didn't think he had much control over height, speed, or just about anything else. His tail curled when he went UP, and his ears flapped out when he went down. His paws just...*pawed* at the air. Soon enough the fear that had gripped him during his first few bounces dissipated, and he found that his noggin had reached the height of the mirror. The other dogs barked their admiration—none of them had ever seen a Lab fly before—but in the background, Finn thought he could hear Alley Cat snicker.

"Now look in the mirror," Sawyer said whenever Finn was facing towards that corner, but up in the stratosphere, it sounded like a howl at first. Finn calmed himself down a little by trying to think of some of the Merriam words he knew, such as candor, egregious, gist, and obsolete. Eventually he could hear his friend clearly, and Sawyer would tell him in which direction he should try to turn. (Finn hadn't been aware that controlling his turning was even an option.) But Finn easily confused his left from his right, and every time he figured it out, he'd forget by lunch, so he took a guess and tried to bounce and turn to his right—and he almost fell out of the air. There was his house! In the reflection, he saw the window and outside of it was his house (or part of it). It looked smaller and like a painting except during one of his bounces, Finn swore he saw Mr. Nutball scurry across the top of the tall wooden fence.

"I see my house!" Finn yelled down. "But how? I'm on a Great Journey."

"The same way that we're here," Becky said. "By the way, I'm acting like I'm not worried. I'm faking the 3 C's."

Finn couldn't tell if his girlfriend was worried or not—he was too worried himself. Sawyer told Becky that she was doing a great job except for telling Finn she was *faking* being the 3 C's: calm, cool, and collected. (This last part Sawyer whispered, but, as previously noted, dogs can't really whisper, so Finn heard every word. Still, it made him feel warm for a moment.)

"What else do you see in the mirror?" Sawyer asked Finn when the black Lab was back in position (facing the round mirror), but he had to bark loudly, for the springs of the bouncy circle were rusted, and they had started to squeak like crazy; the sound filled the overstuffed garage. Sawyer hoped all the noise wouldn't bring out the Big Uns. "Just like my spots, there's always more to see," he said. "At least that's what you guys always tell me."

Finn knew what he meant. Sometimes the two smaller of the three spots on Sawyer, the ones that were lighter, looked like his fur was just dirty there. (Sawyer's absolute most favorite thing to do was to drop and roll in the grass, so maybe that was why, but he avoided rolling in the parts of his yard that had more dirt than grass, so probably not.) But sometimes, when the sun hit those spots, they practically glowed yellow. Finn felt that they even grew warmer when they were at their most yellow, though Becky told him that that was all in his big…

"…noggin! Lift your noggin!" Sawyer barked, and the next time Finn went UP, UP, UP (higher than he'd been thus far), he turned and to his utter surprise, saw his own snout in the mirror.

They'd been in the garage so long, the shadows started to close in. Jim tore after a chipmunk and ended up slipping on a very old strap-on roller skate.

"I'm okay!" Jim yelled from inside a black cloud after crashing into a lonely outside grill. "I thought it was Zach the 'munk."

UP and down went Finn the black Lab, but he was no longer bouncing high enough to see into the mirror. He was getting tired.

"What if gets too dark for Finn to see?" asked Becky. "I could jump with him and help him see…the whole thing," she added, ever fearless.

"What whole thing?" Finn asked as he went UP. Becky obviously knew something that he didn't; he thought only Sawyer knew everything that was going on. What about the *D* word? What about his ears and *SILK*? He did seem to be slowing down a bit.

But Becky had guessed what Sawyer already knew: Finn was the treasure. But the cream-colored Lab had to figure out what the problem was with Finn's bouncing.

Sawyer's snout shot straight up and his sniffer went into overdrive. "Fear," he shouted to his best friend. "Don't worry, Finn: you'll land on your feet when the time comes!"

"I thought that was a cat thing!" Finn shouted back.

From the rafters, Alley Cat's voice floated down, poison on the air. "A cat thing? He's still not seeing it. How much longer do think he can bounce? They didn't make this trampoline with a dog in mind."

Finn hated to admit it, but he was thinking the same thing.

Alley Cat purred: "All he needs is a puddle."

"Okay," barked Sawyer. "Becky, Jim, Alley Cat—everyone quiet. If Finn only has so many bounces left in him, then I need to try to help him see."

All the animals did as they were told. Other than the sounds of nature, all was quiet except for the squeaking of the trampoline. Faintly in the distance, they could hear the WHEET, WHEET, WHEET of the Vicar Pig.

All Finn could think of were those *d*astardly *D* words. He was afraid that he was going to find out rather quickly what 'die' actually meant. (The Vicar's explanations hadn't been much help.) He thought that soon, soon, soon—sooner than he expected—he'd find out what would happen when he "crossed over."

Finn used his legs to gain some height, but he was so weary.

"Try to keep your noggin lifted up," Sawyer reminded Finn.

Again Finn saw his house, the Big Uns' house (or whatever wasn't blocked by the high wooden fence), and again he wondered how could that be. (Of course he didn't know how he ended up in Sawyer's garage with all his friends or how he could hear the Vicar Pig from these great heights; he'd walked over a good deal of the Wold since he'd left the Pig—or so he believed.)

"I see my house! Part of it!"

"What else?"

UP...and down...and UP...and down...

"I see my face! Part of it!"

Sawyer said, "Next time, on your way down, tilt your eyes up, so you're watching the mirror."

UP...and...down...and...UP...and...down...

"Tilting. I don't understand."

"Look up and try to see what remains in the mirror as you do down, if you can"

Now this was a lot for Finn to pull off—all this eye tilting and such—but his Smart Bump didn't let him down. Every time he bounced UP, he'd see (inexplicably) the top part of his (former) house and a bit of his snout. He started trying to see what remained in the mirror as he went down, though he soon didn't have enough altitude for him to see much of anything. He was starting to see only the very bottom of the mirror.

Sawyer noticed this and knew that Becky had been right.

"Everybody get on and bounce!" Sawyer said, but Jim and Becky just stared at him, while Jim tried a little hop. (Alley Cat had split the scene.)

Sawyer sighed. "Do like Becky had said before: everybody get on the bouncy circle, near the edges, and try to bounce, so you catapult Finn up."

"Did you say 'cat' or 'caterpillar'?" the black Lab asked.

" 'Catapult,' my friend!"

"As if," said Mrs. Caterpillar from the top of their branch.

Soon three more retrievers were bouncing—and it worked: they catapulted Finn UP and UP and UP. Finn felt his fur bristle (if he was on the ground, it would have been more visible), for he realized there was another potential problem when he heard chuckling—the mocking kind.

Alley Cat!

From the bouncy circle, Finn looked around the garage for his basketball. He didn't see it anywhere. Wait—there! The ball had rolled into a corner, and in the darkness of that corner, sitting in an old wagon was Alley Cat. Sawyer growled as the feline climbed out of the wagon and approached the ball.

"You get away!" Finn barked rather unconvincingly; one half of his mind was on his orange-and-blue-striped basketball, the other part on his bouncing.

"Keep looking in the mirror, Finn!" Sawyer shouted.

"Leave his basketball alone, cat!" Sawyer bellowed, as he leapt off the bouncy circle.

But Alley Cat appeared not to be afraid of Sawyer. (The other dogs were busy bouncing up and down on their rumps.) He reached the ball at the same as Sawyer, but instead of lunging for it, Alley Cat made a well-aimed kick and before Finn realized it, his basketball was firmly between his jaws.

Sawyer had watched the ball fly through the air, and when he turned around Alley Cat was gone, just some cat hair floating in a lonely sunbeam, but from the shadows, three tennis balls rolled across the garage. Becky and Jim began to clamber off the trampoline before Sawyer stopped them and set them bouncing again.

"I need help here," Finn said, around the basketball.

"Instinct, darling," Becky said by way of apology, as she took a last, longing glance at the tennis balls. She and Jim both released a sigh. Dogs find it difficult to resist tennis balls (and these looked new), a fact that Alley Cat knew all too well. Even Finn, with his beloved basketball in his mouth, wanted to chase after a tennis ball. He even had his eye on one. Only Sawyer's voice broke the spell.

"Let's try this *one more time*," Sawyer said to the retrievers. The shadows were growing long. Soon Finn wouldn't be able to see anything in the round mirror.

Becky and Jim had wide smiles as they bounced.

Finn went UP and down, over and over, circling around every so often. When he was somewhat turned from the mirror, he said (around the basketball), "I can see my house through the window clearer than when I see it in the old mirror."

Sawyer was undeterred. "It's what you see in the mirror that's important."

Finn nodded and tried to turn around again.

In the mirror, he saw his house and his snout. He *still* didn't know how was it possible that he was seeing his house—through the mirror *or* the window—but he was beginning to realize he didn't know a great deal about a good many things.

"Stop wondering how it that you can see your house when you're on your Great Journey," Sawyer barked.

Finn did so. It was difficult.

"What's the last thing you see in the mirror besides your house?" Sawyer shouted.

Finn saw his face again. In his brief look, he noticed that he had significantly more grey on his snout than he thought. He let the basketball drop to the bouncy circle where it took a little bounce of its own and rolled into the shovels. It was risky, but it was hard to bark with it in his mouth.

"I have my eyes on it, my dear," said Becky, perfectly composed.

Jim spoke between bounces: "I'll…retrieve…the ball." (Finn knew his friend couldn't help himself.)

Jim bounced off the trampoline and crashed into the old rakes and shovels. In order to extricate himself from the yard and snow implements, Jim had to break through a couple of spiderwebs, some of which clung to his long coat.

"Well, I never!"said one hairy spider to a hairier one.

"It's okay, Jim, I can see my basketball from here."

"Pay attention to the mirror when you turn back around," Sawyer reminded his pal.

When the golden retriever leapt back on the bouncy circle, the hairier spider, who'd found himself tangled up in Jim's fur, went along for the ride. When Jim started bouncing, the spider-knot came undone, and the spider, whose name was Mr. Twinkle, swung from one of the stray strands.

"Sparkle, help!" cried Mr. Twinkle.

"Mother always said that we should see the world!" Miss Sparkle cried back. "Bon voyage!"

The strand snapped loose, and Mr. Twinkle fell into a sloppily coiled garden hose.

"Oh my," said Miss Sparkle before scurrying towards her brother. "If I told him once, I told him a thousand times: stick to your own kind; don't get stuck on another."

The black mice, now dressed as paramedics, helped Miss Sparkle get Mr. Twinkle up on his eight legs.

Achoo!

"Blesh you!"

Stretch.

"In the mirror, I see my house...I see my face...I'm turning back around."

"Do you see it, I mean the whole thing?" Sawyer asked.

"I see my ears flap a little on my way down...wait: there they are again. My house—my ears! My house—my ears!"

Becky and Jim turned their heads this way and that, looking to see what Finn saw, until Jim looked ill, lost his balance, and went back into the rakes and shovels.

"My house—my ears!" Finn shouted. "My house—my ears!"

"That's it!" Sawyer cried. "Stay with that image: your ears and your house! Remember it!"

The rakes and shovels rattled as an obviously startled Jim ran headlong into the ring of the trampoline.

"E-yow!" barked Jim.

"Are you alright, goofball?" asked a bouncing Becky sleepily.

But before Jim could answer, the Labs' ears perked up at...nothing. The birds had gone silent. The cicadas had stopped whirring. Somewhere in the distance, a father called his son in—but that was it. It was silence broken only by the squeaking of the trampoline's springs. The light seemed to be leaking from the sky outside.

Jim's eyes went wide. "The Realists! It's the Realists!"

But all Finn heard was "The Eel Kiss! The Eel Kiss!" Finn had never met an eel, and he hoped he never would, for in one of the Boy's books that he'd read aloud to Finn, it sounded like eels lived in the water—the one outside the garage apparently did not—and shocked people for a living. The book never mentioned them kissing other creatures. Finn was pretty sure an eel's kisses would be nothing like the Boy's kisses. (Just thinking about being hugged and kissed by the Boy made his heart feel like it was being squeezed by a giant.)

"The Realists! The Realists!" barked Jim again.

So it was the Realists, not Eel Kiss! Finn was relieved, but Becky, who'd been lightly napping while she bounced, opened her eyes and sprung off the trampoline, ready to do battle.

"Go out the way we came in," shouted Sawyer. "We don't want to get trapped in here."

The first two words of Sawyer's next sentence were obscured by Becky's "YEOW!" as she made her way through the opening in the door.

"Splinters," Finn and Sawyer said in the sudden darkness of the garage.

Finn knew that Becky was the bravest of the dogs, so the Realists must be bad. Maybe *this* was what happened when you died.

"Where's my birdcage?" asked a frantic Jim. "I'm going out the way I came in! I'm not—"

From outside the garage, on the side where Jim's window was, there came a hissing and a spitting sound.

"Yikes!" cried Jim has he made his way towards the opening in the garage door, where he was sure to get his long golden hair caught on the jagged wooden sides.

"Careful going—" Sawyer started to stay.

"I'm due for a grooming anyway!" Jim yelled.

RIP!

If the birds and cicadas hadn't left with the arrival of the Realists (at least in the dogs' minds), Finn thought they would have been scared off anyway by Jim's *OUCH, OUCH, OUCH!* Whoever these Realists were (Finn still thought there was a chance they were Kissing Eels), they were enough to send Jim and his long wavy hair right into the teeth-like opening in the garage door. He could see that Sawyer was shivering, and only fireworks and Mr. Boom made Sawyer do that. But before he could ask his best friend who the

Realists were, Sawyer was gesturing with his nose and shouting up to him.

"Bounce sideways!

It was Finn's turn to shiver, but his heart was warm that his best buddy hadn't left him behind to bounce alone and wrestle with the meaning of the mirror (which he could no longer see).

"How do I—?"

"Bounce sideways into me. We're both soft."

Finn did as his best friend suggested and crashed into Sawyer. Then the two of them scrambled for the opening in the garage door where strands of Jim's fur flapped gently in the breeze. Finn grabbed his basketball on the way out and kept his eyes peeled for Kissing Eels just in case, for the last thing he wanted was an Eel Kiss right now.

When they came out of the garage and ducked through a hole in the fence, they ran to a familiar-looking patio. Becky and Jim were gone, and it wasn't as silent as the retrievers had imagined. That still didn't mean that an Eel Smooch wasn't around the corner. A storm was brewing, making it darker still, and the wind was kicking up with some haste.

"You can come in if you want," Sawyer said. Finn knew that Sawyer's Lad would welcome him, but...

"I'm on a Great Journey!" Finn shouted against the wind. "I don't see any eels," he added. He kept one paw on his basketball so it wouldn't fly away.

Finn noticed Becky sleeping under the patio table.

"You don't see any...what?" Sawyer asked, confused. The wind whistled something fierce and the first drops, big fat ones, splattered the Labs.

"I have to keep going on," Finn said, nuzzling his greatest pal. "I have to find the answers to my questions."

"I don't know the answer to your *SILK* question," Sawyer said, "but I know this: you are whatever you are—you can't change it or lose it, even if your tail got cut off or if your ears were made of dandelions. You'd still be a dog. Look at me: I'm a creamy Lab who is really a yellow one; my spots give me away." Sawyer turned in a circle, as the rain continued. "But even though my spots are yellow, I am still a cream-colored Lab."

Sticks and such started flying by. Finn ducked as an acorn came his way. He saw the two black mice clinging to one another before scurrying into the nearby shed. An eye patch and a tiny stethoscope were all that remained, and the wind soon took these to wherever the wind takes such things.

"What did the mirror mean, Tommy?" He was ashamed that he didn't understand.

The wind was howling now. The rain struck the stone patio and began drenching the Labs. Finn could sense that Baron Thunder wasn't far behind, which meant Sawyer could too, which was why he was shivering, but Finn's best friend didn't take off.

"Home is wherever your ears are, and wherever your ears are, well, that's home," Sawyer said. "Sometimes you just have to bring 'em together, just like being adopted brought us to the Boy and the Lad and the Lass and the Little Lady. That's what you eventually saw in the mirror: your ears and your house—you brought them together."

Finn cocked his head. The last few words were lost to the wind, as the rain drops grew fatter and fell in sheets.

"You're a special Lab, you see," Sawyer said, "and if you're special …"

Mr. Boom crackled and shook the very earth. Finn hadn't even seen the lightning. Sawyer shook too but stood his ground as he shouted to Finn: "…if you're special, so are your ears!"

And that was what Sawyer said.

Episode IV

What Turtle Said

Finn woke up and was surprised he was dry. Had he been right? Had he dreamt the adventure in the garage? The trampoline and the pirate mice had seemed so real—not just vestiges of a dream, as Sawyer had suggested. He walked around for hours and hours, it seemed, carrying his basketball in his mouth, keeping his eyes peeled for Alley Cat. Some things looked like things he knew, but that was just his exhausted noggin playing tricks, he told himself. Finn was thinking that he had to be far from home by now—he'd been on the move for so long (naps aside)—when he spied a door and made his way towards it.

The door was made of mostly glass, one of those sliding kinds. (There seemed to be a lot of those.) It looked comfy inside, and to Finn's surprise the door was open. The Great Journey had been an arduous one thus far, and Finn's issues regarding *SILK* were more perplexing than ever. The Vicar Pig had been little help. Pig's Lordy sounded scary and kind of piggish—not at all the loving God Finn remembered from the Boy's *New Picture Bible*. Sawyer had been more help, but it was like he spoke in riddles. No—not riddles: metaphors, another word he'd learned from the Boy and Merriam. He didn't know if he was using it correctly though—he was fuzzy on the definition—but it *felt* right, which he knew didn't count for anything. And what if his adventure with Sawyer and the gang had just been part of a very vivid dream? Then it counted for nothing.

Finn tiptoed into the house (as much as a Labrador retriever could tiptoe) and found a nice spot of sun on the rug. He soon fell asleep, but inside his noggin, in every single nightmare (and he had a bunch right in a row), his ears were on fire, and when he awoke, he shook his head violently to hear them flap; he wanted to make sure they were still there. He didn't sleep very much after that. Finn stayed on the rug in the sunspot near the door (in case this house's Big Uns came along), just staring at his old basketball and remembering much better times.

Can't lose my ears now, Finn thought. They were all he had left in the Wold—besides the orange-and-blue-striped basketball.

"I say, I do say, you there. PFC Huckleberry Finn!"

Finn jumped to his paws. The fur on his neck and back stood straight up in their alert positions. Was it a Kissing Eel? Alley Cat? His mind felt as fuzzy as his belly felt empty. He'd travelled a long way before finding this house (which smelled familiar), resting only when necessary. The basketball had gotten slippery from all the drool, and the road had seemed to go on forever. Plus Finn was still shaken from his encounter with the pirate mice, Alley Cat, and the Vicar. He'd left Pig's place, hoping to find another old acquaintance, Mr. Turtle, who was said to be wise by other animals, but he'd forgotten where he'd seen Mr. Turtle last and had fallen into an adventure with Sawyer. His best friend had told Finn that he was special, therefore his ears were special too, but how special was he if it had all been a dream, one that occurred between his perhaps not-so-special-after-all ears.

And now this: someone calling Finn by his proper name—the name the Boy had given him! Only the Boy and Sawyer (and sometimes Mommy and Daddy Big Un) used his first name.

"*Ahem*! I say, Private Finn! Dog!"

Now that didn't sound as nice.

Finn hoped it wasn't Daddy Big Un (if somehow he'd circled back around). Maybe he'd be in trouble for running away, but more likely he'd be run off the property and told to eat somebody else's shoes. But the truth of it was his Second House was now in the same place his First House was: nowhere. It was sad, but Finn believed this much to be true: once he knew how much his *SILK* was worth, *everyone* would want him in their homes because he would be so valuable. Then, and only then, could he even *think* about maybe, possibly, going back to the Boy and the Big Uns. Of course, by then, the Big Uns would be clamoring for him!

"Finn," the voice said. "I say, Huck Finn."

Now Finn's nose may have been as old as the rest of his body, but as far as sniffers went, Finn thought it top notch (maybe not as good as Sawyer's, but still a solid schnozz), and while Finn didn't completely follow or comprehend the television programs the Big Uns preferred, he thought he would have made a good police dog— as long as there were naps. Finn lowered his big noggin, and his sniffer struck an aquarium, which was smaller than Pig's cage. The aquarium was on a shelf below the Lab's eye level. Disturbingly, he could smell the Vicar.

"Who's there?" he asked.

"Down here, Finn."

Finn positioned his body so he could lower his sniffer into the little aquarium. He instantly regretted the maneuver. If Pig's place had smelled, well, somewhat piggish, this aquarium smelled like— Finn didn't know what. The only reference he could conjure was that one horrible Big Un vacation to Beach Haven, which is where they went just about every summer. One year, galloping on the beach, entertaining the Boy and Daddy Big Un by catching their Frisbee, Finn had paused to investigate a load of seaweed. Finn had been hungry—he was pretty much *always* hungry (he was so, so hungry now, but never mind that, he told himself)—and after a tentative sniff or two, he had sucked the seaweed into his mouth in one gulp. His first thought had been: salad meets bubble gum. Later, when he had thrown up for the tenth and final time that night, with his stomach ginger, and the Boy whispering *SILK* into his ears, Finn swore off bubble gum and salad, and he never went near the stuff again.

The little aquarium smelled just like bubble gum salad—and something (or someone) familiar.

Finn pulled his head out, knocking it on the shelf above.

"Sound the alarm!" the voice cried. "Call the militia! Call the minutemen!"

The top of Finn's noggin HURT. His Smart Bump *t-h-r-o-b-b-e-d*. His Little White Tie raced the devil. For a second (a pretty long time in canine reckoning), he wished the Boy were here to rub his Smart Bump and brush away his crusty tears.

"Did they hurt you, son?" the voice asked. "Are ya hit?"

Finn shook his noggin. He was afraid if he opened his mouth, the voice would hear him cry.

"Are you the scout? The advance man?" the voice queried. "I didn't even know you were one of us!"

Finn wanted to tell the voice that he was no longer one of *anything*—that he was just *one* alone (again)—but he said nothing.

"Or," the voice whispered, "are you *undercover?*"

The *t-h-r-o-b-b-i-n-g* began to subside. Finn cleared his throat.

"I'm not allowed under the covers anymore," Finn said. He didn't know this for a fact, but since he was no longer part of the Big Un family, it seemed a reasonable assumption.

"Whatcha do, Finn? Go AWOL? Frag a sergeant?"

"I ate some shoes," Finn replied.

It hurt just to think about eating the shoes. Finn hoped he never saw another stray pair of shoes his whole miserable life.

"By accident," Finn added, which was true: he'd never meant to chew up the Boy's shoes; they'd just been in his mouth so long... The fact that he had never swallowed any of the shoe leather eluded him. The hyperbole, which overtook his thoughts during the terrible days following the footwear incident, became fact: namely, that he *ate* the shoes.

"Thought they were shoe bombs, eh?" the voice chuckled. "Or were they just your size?"

Finn could hold it back no longer. The bump on his Smart Bump had opened the floodgates, and now tiny pieces of Little White Tie dripped from his eyes. Finn was sure that if he could see his Little White Tie, it would be faded away to nothing.

"I ate the shoes," Finn explained, his words rushing together in a series of quick, short barks, "because I wanted to play basketball and I missed the Boy and he'd been gone a good long time, sir, and I don't remember everything in quite the right order because I don't, and maybe I don't because I just bumped my Smart Bump and the Big Uns, they were mad and—"

"The Big Uns, huh? So you know of the Big Uns?"

The voice was creaky and irascible, alternating between a drawl and a twang.

Finn lowered his head carefully to see the source of the voice. Inside the aquarium, between a bowl filled with lettuce and another, larger bowl filled with water and poop, a bright green rock with oddly shaped panels shifted ever so slightly.

"Yes, I know—I *knew* the Big Uns," Finn responded, for he was nothing if not polite. "Well, Mommy and Daddy Big Un at least."

He wondered who or what was he talking with, which was only natural.

"Sir," Finn began, his leaky eyes momentarily forgotten, "are you a rock?"

"You could say that, private," the rock said proudly. "The rock this great country was built on!"

Finn kept his eyes on the rock. He swore it was moving back and forth!

"How do you know my name, Mr. Rock?" Finn asked.

The rock rocked a bit more, then waddled closer to the side of the aquarium and went POP!

A small, arrow-shaped head stuck out of the big green rock!

"It is I, Finn," the arrow-shaped head said. "It is I!"

"Mr. Turtle!" Finn shouted.

"Shhhh, soldier," Turtle said. "Strictly need to know and all that."

Finn marveled at finally finding Mr. Turtle while on his Great Journey—unless this was still part of the Sawyer dream or maybe a new one. Regardless, it *smelled* real.

The Little White Tie on Finn's chest burned with what the black Lab could only identify as HOPE. Mr. Turtle was exactly the sage Finn's situation needed! The Boy had told Finn, on more than one occasion, that some turtles lived to be a hundred years old. Finn couldn't count to one hundred, but the Boy seemed impressed by the number, so Finn was too. And the past being the past and all, Finn hoped Mr. Turtle understood that he hadn't meant to bother him that morning two summers ago, but the tennis ball Finn had been chasing had taken an odd bounce, and his noggin had followed its bounce into the side of the little aquarium. "Oooh, be careful of the Colonel, Finn," the Boy had said, lifting a green rock into the air. "You'll scare him!"

"Mr. Turtle, sir!" Finn whispered (or tried to).

"Colonel," Turtle corrected.

"It's me, Mr. Turtle," Finn said. "You were right the first time. It's Finn."

Mr. Turtle's head disappeared in a *whoosh*, then POPPED out again.

"Sorry," Turtle said, "had something on the burner. Now, where were we?"

"Well, you called me Colonel, sir, and I said—"

Turtle sputtered and spun in a circle—twice.

Finn sat back on his haunches. Mr. Turtle wasn't very fast. Two complete spins took about a half an hour (give or take ten or twenty minutes; Finn was terrible at time, as was mentioned earlier).

"You, Finn, were not decorated on the Fields of Backyard. I'm the only Colonel here."

"I'm sorry, Mr. Turtle, Colonel sir, I didn't mean—"

Turtle *humpfed* and sputtered and *humpfed* some more.

Boy, Finn thought, do I know how to put my paw in it!

"I do say, Finn, you know how to give a fellow a start," Turtle said in his strange reptilian accent once he'd calmed down.

The Colonel stuck an odd-looking toe in the air. "Back in a flash," he said and *whoosh*: his little head was sucked back into his shell.

Finn scratched an itch.

Finn nibbled on a crumb lodged in the rug.

Finn fell asleep.

"Dog!" Turtle shouted, and Finn snapped to attention. Little wisps of smoke eked out from the neck of Turtle's shell.

"Sir," Finn said, "I think you're on fire." It smelled like meat. "Inside your shell."

Turtle waved his little hand and *pooh-poohed* the thought.

"Just left a roast in the oven too long, son," the Colonel said. "And it's armor, not simply a shell. Had it made special to protect me when the sky starts falling."

"You can cook in there?" Finn asked. (Finn's tongue involuntarily hung out of his mouth; he enjoyed a good piece of meat.)

There followed more sputtering on the part of Turtle (but thankfully no turning).

"Of course, soldier. Full amenities. I'll own the darn thing in two years."

"Own...?"

Turtle ignored Finn.

"What brings you to these here parts?" the Colonel asked, indicating his surroundings slowly (s-l-o-w-l-y) with his arrow-shaped head.

Finn cleared his throat. Asking was always the hardest part.

"Well...mister...sir, I mean...I—"

"Colonel," Turtle suggested (or perhaps it was insisted).

Finn smiled politely. "Thank you," he said.

"You're quite welcome, son," Turtle replied. "My shell is always open to you."

Finn wanted to ask how that was possible but didn't. He had more important things to ask.

"I had a question..."

"Ask away, my boy."

"…but now I have two questions."

The mood in the aquarium changed instantly.

"Oh, you think you'll get away with this?" the Colonel asked. "They'll hunt you down for this, son. Hunt. You. Down. One does not *question* orders. Does one ever *question* the Supreme Commander? Ever? I think not."

Finn dropped his noggin to the floor; the rest of his body naturally followed suit. The Wold made him dizzy.

"Who is the Supreme Commander?" Finn asked, although he was too weary to really care. He'd never heard of a Supreme Commander before, and the identity wasn't of the utmost importance to him. "Do you mean the Lordy?" This, of course, wasn't one of Finn's BIG questions, but he felt compelled to ask.

Turtle's tiny tongue sprung from his pointy mouth then retreated. "The Lordy!?" Turtle screamed.

Finn's eyes were getting heavy.

"Yes, sir. See, Pig said—"

"PIG!" Turtle roared. "The traitor!"

"The Vicar Pig said that if I read the Goodly Book of Goodly Things, then I could go to the Goodly Place—not that I wanted to go. He just sort of told me all on his own."

"Pig," Turtle muttered.

"Cavy," Finn said, though he feared correcting Colonel Turtle.

"Ga-blesh-you, son," Turtle said.

Finn hasn't sneezed, but he thanked the decorated reptile anyway. At least they weren't talking about the Supreme Commander anymore.

Finn sat up. "Mr. Turtle, sir…my questions?"

"Yes, yes," Turtle said. "You came for wisdom, and here I am dispensing tactical advice to a grunt. You may approach the Colonel."

Finn looked around to see if Mr. Turtle was talking to someone else, as the Lab couldn't be any closer to the aquarium. The Colonel had closed his eyes—what sheer little lids he had!—and appeared to be murmuring in his sleep. Unexpectedly, two more sets of eyelids closed; neither were translucent.

"Ask ask ask," Turtle murmured. "Ask."

"The first question is this," Finn said. "What happens when I *die*?"

Turtle's eyelids (all of them) flew open, and he spat and strutted (in a turtle-like fashion). Finn lowered himself to the floor again. He seemed to have a way of setting off his superiors.

"You listen, son, and you listen good," Turtle said. "To *d*ie in battle is glorious. To *d*ie in service to your country is the biggest sacrifice a citizen can make. To *d*ie in the Lordy's name—"

"You said 'the Lordy,' " Finn interrupted.

"Not *Pig's* Lordy," Turtle snapped. " 'The Blanket of the Lordy!' *Pah*! Good God Almighty only helps those who help themselves. There is *not* room for everybody. That...that Pig, his Blanket Theory doesn't hold water. You can't cling to the Blanket Theory. No one will save you, son, if you don't save yourself and your country. Gosh darn pinko Vicar."

"Actually Pig is white and brown and—"

"He's a socialite—nope, that's not it." Turtle mused some. "He's a sociology professor—no, no," the Colonel decided. "He's a social worker, a social butterfly—no, never mind. And never you mind the Blanket Theory, whatever it is."

Turtle's eyes lit up. "Pig is a *socialist*; that's what he is!"

Finn didn't know what that was and furthermore he didn't care. He just didn't want to be impolite. But the Colonel was just getting started.

"To *d*ie in battle is glorious—"

Finn interrupted: "You said that part already."

"Of course, of course." Turtle cleared his throat; he'd become quite phlegmy. "What happens when you *d*ie? That is the question."

Finn sat up and waited. There were long pauses between Turtle's utterances, and he spoke very slowly.

"It's simple," the Colonel said. "If you do the will of the state, why, you go to heaven, son. Lots of dog cookies there, I imagine."

Heaven sounded suspiciously like the Vicar's Goodly Place, but Finn thought better of mentioning it.

"Do you kill baby turtles?" Turtle asked.

"I don't kill anything, sir," Finn said.

"Good, son, good. Killing baby turtles is *not* an activity that will get you into heaven. The Lordy our Good God Almighty says so."

"The Lordy is *God*?" Finn asked.

Turtle stamped his little feet.

"Good God Almighty blesses our country. Good God Almighty gave us this land. Good God Almighty gave us the right to clear the land of all the what-have-yous: the natives, the French, the Mexicans, the gosh darn Redcoats. Basically anyone with a claim to the…well, land. Good God Almighty, Finn, *is* God."

"Good God Almighty," the black Lab repeated. "No killing baby turtles, only what-have-yous."

"Now you're talking, soldier! Now you're cooking with gas!" Turtle shouted in a voice that sounded like it should have been accompanied by a slap on the back. "We kill only the enemy of the day."

Talking with Turtle made Finn's noggin ache again.

"Who is the enemy?"

"The enemy," Turtle responded, "is anybody who threatens our way of life. Essentially, the enemy is anybody *different.* Attack and parry."

"Oh," Finn said, but other than Alley Cat, Finn didn't have any enemies, and Alley Cat wasn't a *real* enemy. (He didn't think the feline was a what-have-you either.) One afternoon, during the previous summer, Finn had spied Alley Cat in the backyard lounging in the sun within striking distance, but the sun was toasty, and Finn, trying to keep one eye peeled (in case Alley Cat tried anything sneaky), lounged the day away as well, not four or five feet away from the tabby.

"What if I don't have any enemies?" Finn asked.

"Terrorists!" Turtle screamed. "What about terrorists?"

"Oh," Finn said again. There was no sense in pretending he knew what a terrorist was.

"And *suspected* terrorists. Got to wipe them out too," the Colonel said. "And animals of the same genus as the terrorists. We can't be too careful. Unless they have something we want. Then we befriend them and attack them later. Or is it the other way around? I don't think it matters. Terrorism gives us the license to do whatever we want in order to protect the state."

Finn didn't want to ask but his natural curiosity got the better of him. "And who are the terrorists?"

"Anybody we say! Good God Almighty will protect us, legally speaking."

Finn thought God must have as many faces and names as Turtle had accents and eyelids.

"Violence is all the terrorists understand," Turtle explained, "and so violence is what we give them. Take those Realists, for example. What we need to do is…"

Finn hung his noggin in defeat. While he wanted to know more about the Realists, he didn't need to hear the battle plans.

"All in Good God Almighty's name, of course," Turtle hastily added.

Finn wasn't sure he wanted to meet this God any more than he wanted to meet Pig's Lordy.

"I hope that answers your question, son," the Colonel said. "Now, if you'll excuse me, I have a roast to baste, a war to plan, and a Vicar to kill."

Finn navigated his snout into the little aquarium. Finn hated being pushy, but he'd come such a long way. Turtle's head disappeared in a *poof!*

"*Hello,*" a mechanical voice said from inside Turtle's shell, "*the Colonel is not currently available to take your call. If you'd like to leave a message, please do so after the long beep.*"

"BEEEEEEEEEEEEEEEEEEEEEEEEEEEEEEEEEEEP!"

Finn wedged his nose underneath Turtle and was about to flip the shell when it occurred to him that the Colonel might not be able to right himself again. Finn extracted his noggin and sat back down. He was not a very happy Labrador retriever. No one wanted to answer his questions. (And Sawyer had been enigmatic—another Merriam word.)

Turtle peeked out of his shell and blinked twice.

"Did you know God spelled backwards is dog, son?" Turtle asked.

Finn sighed. "No, sir," he answered.

"You could be a god. War raises even the lowest among us. War raises us above the struggle of the common man."

"You can come all the way out again," Finn said. "I'm not going to hurt you. I'm sorry if I scared you."

POP!

"Scared, son? Heck, no. I've been in worse campaigns. I remember back in—"

"Excuse me, sir, but could I ask you my other question?"

Turtle smiled—or tried to; turtles don't really smile as much as grin.

"Answered your first query with precision, did I?" the Colonel chortled. "Of course, my dear, dear Finn, ask away."

"Are my ears made of *SILK*?" Finn asked, tilting his head this way and that so Turtle could get a better view of his ears.

"Do *you* think they are?" Turtle responded. "Made of *SILK*?"

If Finn could have turned red, he would have. In truth, Finn was very intelligent (even if he did place more emphasis on retrieving than book-learning), but he was not very Woldly (as noted earlier), despite having lived in two homes since he was taken from his Goner of a mother.

"I don't know what *SILK* is exactly, sir," Finn admitted.

"Exactly!" Turtle cried.

"Exactly?" Finn asked.

"Exactly!" Turtle said. "The freedom to be inexact. That's what we're fighting for! Freedom! Exactly that. At least *our* freedom."

Finn's noggin started throbbing yet again.

"Can I trust you, soldier?" the Colonel asked. "You're not with *him*, are you?"

"Who's *him*?"

Finn wondered what he was getting himself into.

"The Vicar Pig," Turtle said.

"No, we were just talking."

"Did you give Pig an envelope? An offering?"

Finn surely didn't and said so.

"Good, good. Fine, fine. Do you know he doesn't even have a denomination? I hear he doesn't even have a creed," Turtle said. "Here's the toughie, son: did Pig touch you?"

Finn shook his head.

"Good touch *or* bad touch, private."

"No touch, sir," Finn said.

"Fine, fine. Good, good," Turtle said. "The Supreme Commander won't like me telling you this, but if something should happen to me (and let's just hope something doesn't), but if something should, if something did, then I want *you* to carry on with the directive."

Finn missed Sawyer and the other retrievers. The dream Sawyer at least had *something* of an answer to the *SILK* question, even if Finn didn't understand it.

"And if the Vicar Pig did touch you," Turtle added under his breath, "I want you to keep it a secret. Don't ask, don't blab."

Turtle's head *whooshed* back into his shell. Finn could hear clanking and clanging and unzipping and the sound of a motor idling, then shutting off.

"Keep your eyes peeled, soldier," the Colonel said from inside the shell. "Cover me if necessary."

With a *creeeeeeak*, a tiny panel on the side of Turtle's shell opened, and a pale, skinny sliver of liver wearing Turtle's head stepped out. Finn drooled; he enjoyed liver when he could get it.

"I know. Don't say it. I've heard it a million times from the non-coms," the sliver of liver said. " 'How do you keep that body, Colonel?' Let's just say, a little bit of Good God Almighty and a whole lot of supplements—not that you heard it from me."

Finn's mouth hung open. The sliver of liver: it was the Colonel Turtle!

"Go ahead, don't be afraid now, son. Take a look-see," Turtle offered, pointing (as best he could) to the open panel on his abandoned shell. "Snap to it, soldier!"

With a heaping helping of trepidation, Finn lowered his head into the little aquarium and peeked inside Turtle's shell—and what he saw, well, it's safe to say Finn had never seen a carapace like it before. (And while it's also true that Finn had *never* seen the inside of a turtle's shell, the lack of experience took nothing away from his initial wonder and honest appraisal.)

"COOL!" Finn shouted. His bark echoed briefly inside the shell before being dulled by the thick carpets in what Turtle told him was the Sitting Room.

"Soundproofed," Turtle said. "Now, if you'll turn your head to the left, you'll see the Baby Grand and the Picasso above it. And over by the fireplace—just for show, mind you, son; no fires on the ol' plastron—that's an original there; Helmut gave it to me himself. Don't mind the old fashioned answering machine. The dining room table? Sixteenth century. Got the price tag to prove it. Elizabeth I ate her jams sitting right at this table. Never mind those magazines. Someone left 'em here. There—in the breakfront: Ming. The bar? The wood is from a nineteenth-century pirate ship. Shores of Tripoli and all that. Bar's fully stocked, of course. Oh that? Something Versace's boys whipped up for those rare nights out. Three-day pass, you understand. Wink, wink, nod, nod. Now the pool table has to be re-felted, but..."

Now of course, Finn saw none of these objets d'art or creature comforts, but that did little to dampen how impressed he was (though he was a little disturbed at the mention of a pirate ship, whether it was manned by mice or not). He wasn't quite sure, however, how long he could keep holding his head in such an uncomfortable position. He could only look inside Turtle's shell with one eye, and the only way he could get his noggin that low inside the aquarium was to lean against the top edge of the glass. The pressure on his belly was making him gaseous. Any second now…

"…always cleaning. There's no end to it. Had to hire a fire-newt, some lieutenant's nephew. The more stuff you have, the more you want to protect—"

"*PFFFFFT!*" went Finn's heinie.

"INCOMING!" Turtle yelled and dove back into his shell. Finn retracted his noggin and sat back, slightly embarrassed. He hadn't really eaten since he had begun his Great Journey, but his gas still managed to somehow smell like week-old bologna.

"Come in, soldier. Are you there? Over," the Colonel said from inside his shell, making a crackling noise like a walkie-talkie after he spoke: *screeeeeek.*

"Distress signal! Distress signal! Over," Turtle said. "*Screeeeeek.*"

One of Turtle's stubby arms crept out and felt along the ground.

"How many wounded, son?"

Finn inspected his extremities.

"None, sir," Finn reported. "All intact here."

Turtle's head reappeared.

"That was close," Turtle said; he wore a tiny helmet on his arrow-shaped head. "This war is never ending."

"I didn't know we were having a war," Finn said. "Why won't it end?"

"Bad for business if it does," the Colonel said. "If we ended it, how would the military-industrial complex and the defense contractors make money? It's gosh darn unpatriotic. These people have to eat. Buck up, soldier. We're in it for the long haul."

Finn loathed bringing the subject up after such a display of heinie hysterics, but…

"My questions, sir," Finn said in as quiet a voice as a Labrador retriever could muster. "Two of 'em." He figured it couldn't hurt to bring his *D* question back up, since he was getting nowhere with his *SILK* query.

"Are you *d*ense, soldier?" Turtle asked. "I just *d*emonstrated. I just *d*econstructed. I just *d*eclassified."

Finn thought his noggin was going to explode like his heinie had.

"Let me spell it out for you, son," the Colonel said. "Get a writing implement and have your den mother take notes. I'll dumb it down. I'll give you the CliffsNotes version. The Classics Illustrated edition."

Finn shrugged, or at least he thought he did, not out of indifference but because he didn't know what the Colonel was going on about.

"Three words for you, son. Three words. Ready?"

Finn nodded. He had to PFFFFFT again, but he held it in out of respect for Turtle.

"Protect. Your. Neck," the Colonel said.

"Neck," Finn repeated, not wanting to mention that Turtle didn't appear to have done such a great job: when he'd been outside of his shell, the sliver of liver didn't seem to have a neck!

"The Other Party—the Simpers and the Wimpers—they talk about civil *rights* and the Bill of *Rights* and equal *rights*, but they're all Lefties!" Turtle declaimed. "They forget what makes us superior. Yes, yes: race and religion, of course. But they forget what makes us the mightiest and the proudest and the freest: *we have stuff!* Stuff makes us unique. Oh, sure, other countries—Outsiders—have *some* stuff. But we have LOTS of stuff. Heck, we have stuff we don't even need, but if we have it, then nobody else can, and that makes us top dog—no offense meant."

Finn hadn't taken any. But he was intrigued when he heard the word "party." He'd been to the Boy's birthday parties, and weren't they fun? The Big Uns even threw birthday parties for Finn, and they gave him new toys and bones. Why then had they started to act like he didn't exist?

"It's like this, soldier: paw prints, tracks in the snow, droppings," Turtle declared. "If you see a pile of little round poops and some scampering, hesitant tracks, you know the Vicar and his ilk were about. If you see a deep groove in the ground, then, why, that's a turtle! Fingerprints, soldier. They aren't just for clues anymore. Sure, they make us unique. But these fingerprints, as we've learned from scientific advances—the eggheads are good for something—why, that's our *stuff*, son (or some of it). It's a metaphor (I think). We're tied to our stuff; our stuff defines how free we are. Hence, freedom!"

Finn wanted to ask: didn't that mean the Vicar had stuff too? And by "Lefties," did the Colonel mean his enemies were all left-handed? (The Boy was left-handed, Finn knew.) He certainly didn't want to ask Turtle to explain a metaphor (though he would have liked to if only so he would use the figure of speech correctly in the future). Instead he asked: "But aren't there Labrador retrievers and turtles and guinea pigs and stray cats and even goldfish in other countries?" Finn also asked: "Are you saying that the fingerprints of a turtle from another country would look similar to yours?" That didn't sound unique to the Lab. Still, Finn was unaware of other countries, let alone Other Parties, but the Turtle's treatise (a Merriam word, Finn thought) seemed to be in pieces—like a cookie after Finn executed the first chomp—rather than something whole and embraceable like his basketball. He struggled to keep pace.

But Finn believed himself to be an expert on fingerprints, having been read almost all of the Blue Books by the Boy. In the Blue Books, two other boys, Hardy brothers, (junior detectives, the Boy had called them) undertook quests (different from Finn's) and investigated difficult cases. Fingerprints were often involved; droppings were not.

"No! Haven't you been listening, private? Ours are superior because they're *ours!*" Turtle screamed. "We have the *best* stuff! The Outsiders? Bullies! The Other Party? Wimps!"

The Outsiders? The Other Party? Finn wondered who all these animals were.

The Colonel went on with his harangue. "We don't mix our blood with the blood of the Outsiders. We must keep ourselves pure. Labradors with Labradors. Box turtles with box turtles. Even the blood of another turtle species would contaminate…"

But Finn's mind had turned to his basketball. Where was it now? He swore he'd left it next to the sunspot on the rug, but the sunspot had moved to the wall, and Finn didn't see the basketball anywhere.

"Protect what's yours," Turtle continued. "That's it in a nutshell (or any kind of shell). Think our way, and you're one of us. Everything comes down to politics, son, and all politics are local. Your precious *SILK?* My precious shell? I'll tell you: the *SILK* is yours and the shell is mine." Turtle strutted (in a manner of speaking), repeating himself, it seemed to Finn, who was half-listening. "And that's it: freedom, soldier, freedom. We're free because we have the best stuff—and we don't have to share if we don't want to. The Wold: love it or leave it!"

"You just left your shell for a few minutes a little bit ago," Finn said, but he was distracted. Where *was* his basketball?

"Ownership is freedom; consumerism is worship," Turtle said, distracted himself and making little sense. "And I've been back in my shell since, well, since the firefight."

Firefight? Finn sniffed at the rug near the sliding glass door. The basketball had been *right* here…

"It doesn't matter," Turtle said. "With Good God Almighty at our backs—"

"I think someone stole my basketball," Finn said, slumping to the rug. First the Boy, then the basketball. Finn cried softly to himself.

"Bullies!" the Colonel yelled. "The Realists stole your basketball!"

"The Realists?" Finn asked. He still didn't know who or what the Realists really were. Though only a small part of him still believed they were kissing eels, he knew that couldn't be—eels don't have hands to steal a basketball.

"All the Realists are Outsiders of a sort," the Colonel explained, "so all the Realists therefore are bullies."

Finn followed the logic (somewhat) and didn't like where it led.

"Who are they?" the Lab asked.

"I don't know who the Realists are. It's all very cloak and dagger, son."

"But how could you know it was them if you don't know what they are?"

"It smells like one of their capers," the Colonel said.

Finn began thinking that he wanted out of this particular dream—with his basketball.

"Look!" Turtle said, pointing (as best he could) with his tiny stub of a hand. "The door to the Other Country is wide open!"

"The Other Country…?"

"Pa-Ti-O," Turtle whispered. "Then the Fields of Backyard."

Finn sighed. He missed his bed and the Boy and the Boy's Blue Books.

"The time for subtlety is over!" the Colonel stated. "Here—reach in and stick a paw right there on the edge of my shell. Flip me like a tiddlywink."

Finn did as instructed. Turtle went *FLIP!*

"Good job, soldier."

It was Turtle's voice Finn heard, but where was Turtle? Finn spun around.

"I can't see you, Colonel," Finn said. "Did you *d*ie, sir?"

"I am on your back," Turtle said. "Safety in numbers, son. Together we'll ride towards our *d*estiny. Together we'll rescue the basketball from the bullies, those Realists, and *d*ecimate their ranks once and for all. I'll be directing the campaign, of course, so I'll need a ham radio, a deck of cards, a couple of number two pencils..."

Finn looked at his reflection in the sliding glass door (careful not to look at his wretched ears despite his adventure with Sawyer). Turtle was indeed on his furry back. How odd: although Turtle wasn't wearing a Colonel's hat or a helmet of any kind, Finn watched him in the reflection adjust some headgear nonetheless. The Colonel dug his feet into Finn's back like he was spurring a horse (which was annoying), but thoughts of the basketball kept Finn focused on the task at hand.

"Now is the time," Turtle said, "for heroes and for ghosts, for might for right, four score and seven years ago..."

Finn heard it first: *THWACK!*

"My basketball!" Finn cried, and indeed, once Turtle piped down, Finn was sure the Colonel could hear it too.

THWACK! THWACK! THWACK! THWACK!

Someone was dribbling Finn's basketball!

"Charge!" Turtle yelled.

"Basketball!" Finn barked. He leapt through the open sliding glass door and landed on the stone patio. To the right was the dogwood tree and a gate; to the left was a very still earthworm and beyond the patio: the Fields of Backyard. Finn galloped to the left.

"Tippecanoe and Tyler too!" Turtle cried.

And then: nothing. The backyard was empty. No *THWACKING.* No basketball.

"It's a setup!" Turtle yelled. His beak was chattering, as he took in the empty yard. "It's an ambush. It's a doomsday scenario. Pull out your *New Picture Bibles*, men!"

One short whistle. One long. Another short.

"They're using code to call more troops," the Colonel said. "We're outnumbered, out-manned, out-whistled—"

"Shhh," Finn said.

One short whistle. One long. Another short.

And there, perched atop the tall wooden fence surrounding the patio and backyard, was a small muscular tabby with emeralds for eyes and a tail that appeared to have its own agenda.

"Alley Cat," Finn said, nodding his head in greeting.

Turtle tried to burrow into Finn's fur.

"Huckleberry, I presume," Alley Cat replied. "We meet again."

"Why don't you come down from there?" Finn suggested. He was anxious to recover his basketball (which the cat did not appear to have on his person).

"You know why," Alley Cat said. "If I come down, then you have a better chance of catching me."

"You're fast," Finn said. "Aren't you?"

Alley Cat imitated Finn's bark: rough on the outside, maple syrup on the inside. Finn was pretty sure he was being made fun of and didn't like it one bit.

"So we're at an impasse, you and I," Alley Cat said.

WHEET! WHEET! WHEET! WHEET!

"That sounded like Pig," Finn said to the Colonel, but Turtle had retreated into his shell and did not seem to be currently accepting any calls.

"A protester," Alley Cat said with a laugh, jerking his head towards the WHEETS.

"I want my basketball back," Finn said. "Did you take it?"

"And if I did?" Alley Cat hissed.

"The basketball's mine, cat, and I've had it forever. I came to the Big Uns' house with it. I could have even had it on the farm. I should have kept a better eye on it, but—"

"Woulda," Alley Cat said.

"Coulda," Alley Cat continued.

"Shoulda," Alley Cat concluded.

The fur on Finn's neck and back stood at attention. He bared his teeth and growled low in his throat.

"Is that a growth on your back?" Alley Cat asked.

"A growth?" Finn replied, trying to peek behind him. Was this a cat trick?

"Oh, you mean—"

"Keep it down, soldier," the Turtle's shell whispered.

"But I thought the time for subtlety was over," Finn whispered back, loud enough, of course, for Alley Cat to hear.

"A tactical retreat is *not* subtle," Turtle's shell said. "We need reinforcements."

Finn blinked. He wondered if Sawyer lived in this part of the Wold.

"What about the earthworm?" Turtle's shell suggested.

Finn, using a phrase he'd learned from Daddy Big Un, said, "He looks like he's down for the count."

"We could attack *him* then," Turtle's shell said.

There was a loud rustling noise on the other side of the wooden fence, as if some creatures were climbing it. Since dogs don't climb, not like this, he knew it wasn't Sawyer, Becky, and Jim.

"Oh my," Turtle's shell said. "Sit!"

Finn, who'd attended a number of obedience classes, descended into a sitting position. Turtle's shell slid slowly down his back.

"Obligations," Turtle said. The Colonel's feet appeared and the very tip of his beak protruded from the front of his shell. "We're out of supplies."

Three more felines had lined up on top of the wooden fence on either side of Alley Cat. They were much larger than Alley Cat, but they seemed to treat him with deference.

"Shoulda," Alley Cat said, pointing to his left. A fat orange tabby nodded his head in Finn's direction.

"Left the water on," Turtle muttered to himself, crawling back towards the open sliding glass door.

"Coulda and Woulda," Alley Cat concluded, gesturing to his right. Coulda was an older Siamese wearing a black eye patch (a bigger version of the one worn by a certain pirate mouse). Woulda— well, it was hard to see just what kind of feline Woulda was. Woulda was a huge ball of grey fur with a tail where his nose should be! A monster cat perched precariously on the fence!

"Backwards again!" Alley Cat said, rolling his eyes.

Coulda nudged the gray monster. Woulda apologized and turned around in great haste, lowering a bandit mask over his face. (Finn recognized it as one of the masks abandoned by Sawyer and company in the garage.) The black Lab was thankful that Woulda had a rather normal face after all.

"I'm looking for my basketball," Finn said. "It has orange and blue stripes. Have you seen it? Any of you?"

All four cats began strutting in unison along the top of the wooden fence. They flicked the back of their necks with their claws like they were flipping up collars on leather jackets (or so Alley Cat explained). All four strays (for none of them had homes) began wiggling their front paws, as if they were snapping their fingers like the Jets and Sharks from *West Side Story*, but their faux snapping made no sounds that Finn could hear.

"No opposable thumbs," Alley Cat said by way of explanation and shrugged. Cats are good shruggers.

Finn understood the problems that came with not having opposable thumbs. Though sympathetic, he didn't let his guard down.

"Are you a gang?" Finn asked.

"A bevy," Woulda said, and Coulda knocked him off the fence with a well-aimed swoop of his tail.

"Despite our fantastical notions and the exertions of my compadres," Alley Cat said, "we prefer to call ourselves the Realists."

"The Realists!" Finn said to himself. No eels involved whatsoever. The word fit comfortably in his mouth—despite having originated from a cat (though truthfully he'd first heard it from Echo). So these were bullies, according to the retreating Colonel.

Finn thought he heard barking from the other side of the fence— Sawyer!—but then it stopped. It was getting mighty hard to tell what was a dream and what was—

"Jumping Jehoshaphat!" the Colonel shouted as he peeked back (no small feat for a turtle). "*They're* the Realists!"

It was taking Turtle a long time to reach the sliding glass door; not only was he very slow, but he kept stopping to withdraw into his shell.

Woulda climbed back to the top of the wooden fence and attempted to adjust the collar on his imaginary leather jacket. Woulda's neck looked like it was surrounded by two imaginary black wings.

"If you're going to join in our exploits, Huckleberry," Alley Cat said, "then you'll need to become a Realist too. Or, if you prefer the Groucho method, we'll grant you membership without you actually joining.

"Groucho?" Finn asked.

"Groucho Marx, a Big Un," Alley Cat responded. He said: 'I refuse to join any club that would have me as a member.' Realists, of course, know there's safety in numbers (even Turtle knows that), but we accept that each of us *dies* alone. The price of freedom."

Finn scratched himself. There was that *D* word again. He hadn't been planning on joining any gangs during his Great Journey nor had he expected to be asked (if that was what was happening). But still— safety in numbers, just like all the retrievers in his dream, dogs that weren't in this part of the Wold it seemed; if they were, they must all be inside now, even Jim the escape artist golden retriever. If Finn was home, he could be amongst the other dogs, and Sawyer would lead them on yet another adventure (which the Lab thought was most likely very different from Alley Cat's *exploits*). But Finn had to admit that unlike Sawyer he didn't have a compass inside him or a map on his back to navigate (all alone) the scary Wold far from the Big Uns' house. All Finn had was his Little White Tie, which was pounding out a furious jungle beat, plus his whiskers, which were twitching like mad.

"Are with us," Alley Cat asked, "or are you against us?"

Shoulda the orange rotund tabby crept along the fence until he flanked Finn. Finn kept his eyes on Alley Cat. Coulda the Siamese climbed down the fence and circled the Lab.

"What's it gonna be, Finn?" Alley Cat asked. "Are you ready to open your eyes, or do you prefer to trip around in darkness the rest of your life?"

Turtle popped his head out.

"Don't listen to him, soldier," the Colonel hissed. "They're Realists! They see things *as they actually are*! They do things because they *like* them. They mix ketchup and mustard. They believe that if it looks green, then it probably is. They want to hold the government accountable for its actions. They believe that it matters more how you live your life than which deity you bow down to."

Shoulda and Coulda moved suddenly until they stood on either side of Turtle.

"They like the fat Elvis as well as the skinny one," Turtle said, "and they believe in climate change!"

Coulda raised his arms straight up in the air and ducked his head. Shoulda stepped backwards a few paces and squinted his jeweled eyes.

"They think the Constitution is stronger than any one person!" Turtle yelled to Finn.

Shoulda took a running start, and his left hind leg connected with Turtle, who was too far into his diatribe to retreat into his shell in time.

"They eat French food!" Turtle yelled, as his head and stubby legs flapped in the air, easily clearing Coulda's raised-arm-goalposts.

"Not again!" Turtle cried, as his shell sailed over the wooden fence and plopped into the next yard—Sawyer's kingdom, if the cream-colored Lab actually lived there.

Shoulda took a victory lap. Coulda spiked an imaginary ball. Woulda jumped up and down, waving an imaginary pennant, before taking a header off the fence, and landing, snout first, in a pile of leaves.

"Don't worry," Alley Cat said, as he danced along the top of the fence. "We'll bring the Colonel back eventually. Only his ego is bruised."

Finn could hear Turtle yell from the other side of the fence.

"They believe love is all you need! They want to give peace a chance! They never buy lottery tickets! They will soil your *SILK*!"

And that was what Turtle said.

Episode V

What Alley Cat Said

Finn was a Goner.

Alley Cat leapt to the long, twisted bough of the dogwood tree. Coulda and Shoulda closed ranks and stood behind Finn, so close he could smell tuna fish on their breath. Woulda, the big ball of grey, extracted himself from the pile of leaves, marched across the patio, and planted himself (backwards) a few feet from Finn's twitching whiskers.

Finn willed the fur on his back to stand at attention again, but the anger wasn't there. Oh, the fear was—but not enough fear to fight. (Maybe being a Goner wasn't so bad…but no.) What Pig and Turtle had said had confused him at first—but, truthfully, what they'd squeaked or grunted helped begin to clarify Finn's thinking, but the Lab wasn't yet aware of these clarifications. On the one hand (or paw), he saw the feline Realists in their imaginary matching leather gang jackets as a death squad and felt quite ready to surrender. On the other hand (or paw), even though he was a retriever, not a fighter, he didn't give up easily.

"Can I please have my basketball back?" Finn asked, his voice barely above the buzz of a bee.

"Shoulda," Alley Cat commanded. "The basketball."

Shoulda waddled past Finn and climbed over the fence. Time passed, as everyone stood around, trying not to look at one another. Alley Cat checked his imaginary watch a couple of times. A few minutes later the basketball flew over the fence and hit Woulda on top of his head.

"You're just giving it back to me?" Finn asked.

"It's yours, isn't it?" Alley Cat answered. Shoulda climbed back over the fence in time to see Woulda wander in a woozy daze and come to rest in the yard, face down, inches away from a pile of dog excrement. The basketball rolled away. Finn tried to stay put. He had questions.

"Who are you?" Finn asked.

"You know who I am," Alley Cat said.

"I think I do," Finn barked. "I thought I did."

"Stop conjugating, Huckleberry," Alley Cat mewed. "Say what you mean."

"Are you Lordy?" Finn asked. "Or...or Good God Almighty?" He thought of something else, which he believed was reasonable to ask, seeing how Alley Cat was most definitely in charge. "Are you the Supreme Commander?"

Alley Cat laughed. Shoulda and Coulda giggled too. Woulda snored next to the pile of dog feces. A tired fly, who'd been buzzing the poop, took a brief respite on Woulda's nose.

"Who are you?" Finn asked again, deeply embarrassed. Even though he wasn't very Woldly, he wasn't aware of not being Woldly. Until his recent adventures, Finn thought life revolved around loving and being loved. Religion, politics, Leonard Bernstein musicals— these things occupied little space in the places between his whiskers and his Smart Bump.

"Count Bjørn de Vagabond," Alley Cat said, introducing himself and bowing deeply—but not so deep that he fell out of the dogwood tree. Shoulda and Coulda bowed too. Woulda snorted in his sleep, scaring the fly. He rolled over twice, his face still in the grass, and his snoring actually got louder.

Finn never knew that Alley Cat had a real name—and he had *no* idea that the cat was a count. He bowed deeply before something tugged at his brain.

"What does the *D* stand for?" Finn asked apprehensively.

"The *D*?" Alley Cat replied.

Finn nodded. "The *D*." It seemed as if *D* words were everywhere.

"As in, '*de* Vagabond,' " Finn continued.

Shoulda and Coulda guffawed until Alley Cat whistled sharply.

"The *D* in my name, Huckleberry?" Alley Cat asked. "*D*angerous."

I already knew that, Finn thought. Then came the litany of *D* words.

"*D*elightful, of course. *D*electable even. *D*espicable too. *D*ecidedly *not* *d*astardly—though all the lady cats might *d*isagree."

Shoulda nodded gravely. Woulda curled up into a ball and snored into his armpit. Shoulda tried to keep the flies off his sleeping furball of a friend, then gave up and took his place next to Coulda.

"What else, what else? *D*ependable. *D*emonized—at least by your kind, aye Huckleberry?"

Finn nodded, but it was more of a nicety than an affirmation. Woulda had just rolled into the dog poop. None of the other Realists paid attention.

"*D*epraved," Alley Cat continued. "But only on a *d*are."

Shoulda and Coulda snickered.

"And when it rains: *d*amp," Alley Cat said. "Oh, can't forget this one: *d*evilish. The *D*evil of Mondauk—a sobriquet conferred by the felines feminine. I could go on forever with bad *D* words, even some good or innocuous ones. But really '*de*' in my name just means I came from somewhere called Vagabond, which is a place full of tramps like me."

Woulda snapped awake and sniffed at his chest; his grey fur was caked with poo. He stretched out his little tongue-comb, but Shoulda reached him first and conked Woulda on the head. Coulda ran over to join the violence, slipped in the poop, and skidded headfirst into the wooden fence.

"Of course, only one *D* word matters in the end, dear Huckleberry. You know what that word is, don't you?" Alley Cat asked.

Finn tried to concentrate on *D* words. He wasn't sure if "dog cookies" was one word or two—and either way, how could "dog" be a bad *d* word? (Then again how could *d*amp or *d*electable be bad? He had a feeling Alley Cat was teasing him with *D* words, and he didn't care for it.)

"Bologna?" asked Shoulda, rubbing his considerable tummy. "That a *D* word?"

Coulda smacked Shoulda's nose with Woulda's tail.

"I'll tell you," Alley Cat said, leaping to a lower branch. "Death. That's the last *D* word, the final one, and when it comes, there's a good chance you won't even know it because you'll be *d*ead."

"*D*ead," Finn repeated. "*D*eath." He didn't like the way the words tasted in his mouth. Just thinking of dog cookies had made him think of the Boy and the Boy's bed and the stuffed animals and the Blue Books—and, yes: dog cookies. But: *d*ead…*d*eath…

Shoulda pointed to a spot on Coulda's dusty, golden chest, and when the Siamese cat looked down, Shoulda flicked him under his chin with his paw. Coulda was so surprised, he fell backwards and smacked his head on the fence again.

"Isn't that one of your big questions, or was it something more specific when it came to *d*ying?" Alley Cat asked. "I believe the Vicar Pig led you down this *d*ark alley."

"Yes!" Finn barked. "I only had one question when I started my Great Journey, but now I have *three* questions.

"What happens when I *d*ie?

"What is freedom?

"And are my ears made of *SILK*?"

"What happens when you *d*ie? That *is* specific." Alley Cat sighed. "Some things are better left to the learned. Most would do better, at times, to remain ignorant. But I can tell this is not to be."

Coulda wandered back from the yard, rubbing his noggin; he appeared to be cultivating his own Smart Bump. Shoulda was in stitches; anything that involved cartoonish violence struck the orange tabby as very, very funny (unless it happened to him, of course). Shoulda laughed so hard at the Siamese's misfortune, he farted. Coulda forgot all about his injuries and farted back. Woulda turned quietly on his side to try to clean the dog poop from his stomach surreptitiously, but he caught a whiff of his fellow Realists and ripped one in sympathy. (Truth was, Woulda was always passing gas, so this was just an excuse. Woulda's toot was a little one, but he felt an even bigger one coming.)

"Boys!" Alley Cat said sharply, and the Realists fell into formation and began attempting to snap in unison. When this failed, the Realists instantly forgot the Count's reprove. Coulda's head had little bloody scrapes from his encounters with the fence, and Shoulda tried to administer First Aid with help from the black mice, now dressed as doctors with little white coats and tiny stethoscopes. (They'd been waiting in the wings for just the right time to make their entrance; mice had to be quite careful around cats.) Woulda covered his poo-plastered tummy with his paws. His face was twisted with effort and strain, as he tried in vain to hold it in, for he knew it would be a bad one, but…

RRRIPPP!

The Realists fell about themselves and into the excrement. Alley Cat waited until they had recovered, cleaned themselves as best they could, and assumed formation before returning to the subject at paw.

Finn said covered his nose and said "The Vicar told me I had to read the Goodly Book of Goodly Things in order to go to heaven when I *die*. He said I couldn't be…"

Finn couldn't remember.

"Oh, we can help you here, can't we, boys?" Alley Cat laughed.

"Jewish?" Coulda asked. "Sikh?"

"Muslim?" Woulda asked. "Christian?"

"Black or brown or any 'unacceptable' color?" Shoulda asked, eyeballing the Lab. "No offense, Finn."

"None taken," said Finn, the very black Labrador retriever (with the Little White Tie).

"Right," Alley Cat said. "Racial purity is baked into Turtle's and Pig's Worldviews, but fearing and hating creatures that are different, well, it's not just the cavy's and the reptile's purview, which brings us back to religion. See, it's not just following the rules of the Vicar's Goodly Book that will get you into heaven, as the Pig claims. No, it's following the *Vicar's* rules. That's what he wants."

"For…" Coulda began.

"…he is…" Shoulda said.

"…the conduit…" Woulda continued, surprising himself and his comrades by pronouncing "conduit" correctly. Shoulda and Coulda pounded him on his back.

"…of the Lordy," Alley Cat concluded, smiling.

Finn scratched an itch and shook his ears: he needed a second to think.

"The Vicar Pig believes in the Lordy, and Colonel Turtle believes in Good God Almighty," Finn said.

"Same difference," Alley Cat explained. "They *demand* that you live *their* way. Imagine the kind of life that has time to protest gay marriage. What does the most popular Goodly Book say, Coulda?"

"There's more than one Goodly Book?" Finn asked.

Coulda asked, "Do you want one in Latin or a more modern interpretation?"

"Just whatever you have at hand," Alley Cat responded.

Coulda produced an imaginary Gideon's Bible with a red cover from a hidden pocket (that he didn't have) with a flourish. " 'Judge not, that ye be not judged,' " Coulda read.

"Matthew 7:1," Coulda added. The Siamese fell back into formation and slipped in Woulda's mess, losing grip of the imaginary

Gideon, which flew out of his paw, grazing Mr. Nutball, who'd been trying to sneak by the conclave.

"Well, I'm judging!" said a quite annoyed Mr. Nutball. "Imaginary or not!"

"See, Pig wants you to live according to *his* book," Alley Cat said. "If you're gay, you're *d*amned. If you believe in another *d*eity, you're *d*amned. Hell of a *D* Word: *d*amned. Don't misunderstand me: the way *is* narrow, but its narrowness has NOTHING to do with ministers and imams and rabbis and popes and following the letter of the Goodly Books (and there are many). It's all about how you live your life. Nothing more. Nothing less."

"But Pig said we were all protected under the blanket of the Lordy," Finn said.

"Would you jump out of a window with only a blanket for a parachute?" Alley Cat asked.

"No, but—"

"No buts," Alley Cat said, and Woulda, Coulda, and Shoulda collapsed in a pile of chortles, covering up their rear ends. "In a situation of unbearable fear, you might reach for the Blanket. But the Blanket doesn't do anything in and of itself, other than keep you in the dark, which is what many (but not all) peddlers of Goodly Books want: a congregation in the dark. There are good men and creatures of God out there, but they are harder to find than you'd think. But *d*ying is a big deal with every belief system."

"Have you read the Vicar's Goodly Book of Goodly Things?" Finn asked.

Alley Cat scaled the trunk of the dogwood to reach the next branch.

"Sure have. Know thy enemy," Alley Cat said. "There is a reasonable amount of wisdom in Pig's Goodly Book, to be fair. Even the parts of the Goodly Book Pig's ancestors tossed out (no *d*issenting theologies allowed) have passages that will make your Little White Tie thunder and swoon."

Finn ducked his noggin to try and see his Little White Tie. As usual, he could not, and he looked back up, slightly *d*isappointed. Shoulda waddled over, all smiles (as if he had seen something the Lab had not), and pointed to Finn's chest, and when Finn looked down again, Shoulda smacked Finn under his chin. (Shoulda loved doing this.)

"Fellas!" Alley Cat said before Finn could even start to growl.

"I still don't understand," Finn admitted, keeping a stern eye on the rest of the Realists (so stern, he lost track of his basketball.)

What happened next burned beneath Finn's Smart Bump for years after, for the sky didn't *grow* dark—it was more like someone turned the lights out. Shoulda banged on a piece of tin: THUNDER. Coulda stood in front of Finn (a few feet away, just in case) and blinked his eyes, open and shut, open and shut: LIGHTNING. Woulda ran behind Finn and spit into the air: RAIN.

There appeared in the middle of the backyard a pile of bones, and on top of the pile, spun Alley Cat. No, not *spinning* as much as *dancing*. As Alley Cat danced (and Coulda blinked, Shoulda thundered, and Woulda spat), a bunch of bones shook loose from the pile and scattered across the backyard. What followed was the most amazing spectacle that Finn had ever seen: the scattered bones scurried towards one another and joined up with a terrible CLICKING. Once they were satisfied with their appearance (some of the more astute bones helped the littler bones build themselves), they danced in a circle around the pile: clacking and creaking, shimmying their bone bodies, raising their bony paws to the dark sky, bowing their skulls to the suddenly cold earth beneath their bony feet. Cat skeletons!

Shoulda, Coulda, and Woulda cheered and mewed encouragements. Alley Cat raised his paws towards the heavens, and in the last crackle of Coulda's lightning, fell into pieces and melted into what remained of the pile of bones. The cat skeletons followed suit. Finn wouldn't have believed what was happening if he wasn't seeing it. (He wished Sawyer was here and not for the first time.) The backyard went silent except for the rattle of bones as the remains of Alley Cat and the cat skeletons settled into the center of the pile.

Finn shut his eyes. Alley Cat has just *died*—right in front of him. Finn regretted all the times he'd chased Alley Cat and barked at the Count. Finn's eyes were soaked, and the tears traveled the length of his snout to hang off the end of his already-runny nose.

Shuffle shuffle shuffle.

Finn shut his eyes even tighter. *D*eath had come for Alley Cat. Surely, it wouldn't pass up an opportunity to add Finn to its pile of cat bones, even though he was a dog.

Then something soft tickled his nose. Finn's Little White Tie pounded (*ba-BOOM, ba-BOOM, ba-BOOM*) until Finn's chest was its own thunderstorm.

"Blow," Coulda said.

Finn dared a peek: Coulda was holding Shoulda's tail and using it to wipe tears off the Lab's snout. (Shoulda giggled, for Finn's whiskers tickled.) The lights had been turned back on. The sun painted the part of the backyard it couldn't reach in shadows. The pile of bones was gone. Alley Cat was now in the sycamore tree, grooming himself. The other Realists had returned to the patio. Woulda used fallen dogwood leaves to wipe the remaining poo from his tummy.

"And that," Alley Cat said as Finn blew his nose into Shoulda's tail, "was the *Dance* of the *Dead* Cats."

Episode VI

What Transpired After the Dance of the Dead Cats

"The *Dance of the Dead Cats*," Finn whispered to himself (which is to say, he spoke aloud).

"Did you like it?" Coulda asked.

"We worked all summer on making it more modern," Shoulda said between giggles.

"I was the one spitting," Woulda said, wiping the excess off himself. "I played Rain."

Finn opened his mouth, but nothing came out.

"That was *Death*, Huckleberry," Alley Cat said. "The last of the *D* words. Not very pretty, but still somehow beautiful."

Finn thanked Shoulda, Coulda, and Woulda, who backed away, bowing their heads.

"I don't pretend to know what happens when cats—or dogs or pigs or turtles—*die*," Alley Cat said. "Maybe one of the Goodly Books is right. Maybe there is a judgment day, and every little thing you've done, everything you've stolen, will be accounted for. But if there is, and you've lived a pretty good life, does it matter if you ate meat on Friday or forgot to bow to Mecca one afternoon? I just don't know."

Coulda and Shoulda looked at one another and began emptying their imaginary pockets of all sorts of very real booty (some things just can't be explained): soda pop bottles, a can opener they could never use because of their lack of opposable thumbs, a couple of tennis balls, half a bologna sandwich (an awkward grin crawled across Shoulda's puss), the pair of black mice now dressed like astronauts (who exited the scene hastily with the remains of the bologna sandwich), the soundtrack album to *West Side Story*, and lastly, from Coulda's deep pocket: Finn's orange-and-blue-striped basketball! The Lab could barely believe it: the basketball was glowing just the slightest bit, as if someone had lightly scattered Faerie dust over it.

Finn's stomach had started growling at the mention of meat on Fridays and had gone into overdrive when he saw the half of a bologna sandwich—it had been a while since he'd eaten anything, and he seemed to have caught a cold, probably from sleeping on the air conditioning vent before his encounter with Pig—but when Finn caught sight of the basketball, Little White Tie's tempo doubled and drowned out his stomach and made him forget his cold..

"See, when you *die*—when any of us *die*s," Alley Cat continued, "all that happens is that we change. Change is scary. We like what is comfortable. If things change too much or too fast, we grow scared and jumpy. We cling to ideologies and religions (and maybe rightly so) to help us explain why things change. But change is the only thing that doesn't change."

Finn listened, but seeing his basketball (again) after his long Great Journey made Little White Tie hurt more than expected. Finn thought of the Boy and how the Boy would whisper to Finn before they both fell asleep. *A Lab's ears are made of* SILK. He remembered the Boy rubbing Finn's tummy and feeding him cookies, and the two of them shaking hands and playing basketball and snoozing under the warm, warm sun.

"What happens after we *die* is none of our business," Alley Cat said. "We're no longer. That is the only truth. The Goodly Books and Sutras go on endlessly about it, but they are too concerned with rules and regulations and rituals. Religion concerns itself with the possible outcomes of how you live your life; it concerns itself with where you might *go* after you expire."

Alley Cat looked around. "But if there's more than this, then…"

The Count shrugged.

"But what if I didn't live a good life?" Finn asked. "The Boy and the Big Uns were so mad at me because I was bad."

"And what was your sin?" Alley Cat asked.

"Shoes," Finn sighed.

"You wore the Boy's shoes?" Coulda asked.

"No," Finn replied. "I ate them." He looked down at his paws. "Well, I chewed them. I only swallowed little bits, but that was by accident."

"I ate a pair of Converse once," Woulda said, "and the laces got all entangled inside my tummy, and when I pooped—"

"Is that all?" Alley Cat asked, speaking to Finn (but glaring at Woulda, who sulked away and put his bandit mask back on, which he'd taken off for the *Dance of the Dead Cats*). "No more sins?"

Finn tapped into his Smart Bump. Gosh, there were so *many* sins—if sins were what bad behavior was called. Finn's whole life was one big sin! Bad dog!

"I bullied Turtle," Finn admitted.

"Is that so?" Alley Cat asked, with a smile playing on his face.

"Yes. Turtle said all cats, Realists anyway—begging your pardon, Count Bjørn—were bullies, and that's why he had to wage war on you. But I bullied Turtle into his shell!"

Alley Cat laughed. "That's a pretty grave sin there, Huckleberry, but you don't go around bullying turtles in general, do you?"

"He's a colonel—but no!" Finn barked.

"I only know one turtle," Finn added as an afterthought. "And I think the Colonel might be him. It's confusing."

Alley Cat descended from the sycamore and sashayed over to Finn.

"We're all bullies once in a while," Alley Cat explained. "The Goodly Books have it wrong. *Bullying* is the original sin. The trick is to not do it quite so often if you can help it. We're all animals, Huckleberry. Some animals eat other animals. Some people stomp on ants. There's a difference. Lions and tigers and bears (oh my!) have to eat, and the antelope are aware of this, so the Lordy or Good God Almighty or Whomever (the Is, if you will) gave the antelope strong, powerful legs so they can try to outrun its predators. The antelope, of course, are not particularly pleased with the situation, but they understand, in their Little White Ties, to borrow a phrase, that the ultimate *D* word, *d*eath, is inevitable and that lions and tigers and bears (oh my!) are just being true to their nature. But if we try to remember to curtail the kind of bullying that hurts other animals for no reason (like stomping on ants)—why then: when our time comes to *change*, we can ascend the pile of bones free from original sin (or least free enough)."

Alley Cat cleared his throat.

"All this speechifying has left my throat dry," the Count rasped. "Could one of you please…?"

Coulda and Shoulda had paid no attention to Alley Cat's *d*eath *d*issertation and were busying themselves bouncing Finn's basketball off Woulda's noggin.

"Never mind," Alley Cat said, making his way towards a puddle.

Finn watched the Realists play basketball. He wondered if they'd let him join in (seeing how it was his ball).

"Which brings us to freedom," Alley Cat said when he finished quenching his thirst. "Your second question, I believe. *D*eath, then freedom."

Finn tore his eyes from the game. If he could get his basketball back, then maybe…

No, it was better not to think about the Boy too much. The Boy probably thought Finn was *d*ead. And if so, did he care?

"What is freedom?" Finn asked. "Turtle said that's why our country's better than other countries. We're free because we have better stuff—or something like that."

"Been to many countries, have you?" Alley Cat asked. Coulda and Shoulda leaned closer to hear Finn's answer. Coulda, in particular, being Siamese, felt that Wold travel was in his blood—and relayed this thought to Finn. Woulda chased the astronaut mice around the backyard.

"Well, no," Finn answered, "but the Colonel, I think, believes that inside and outside are different countries. I've been to both." Finn paused. "Turtle didn't make much sense sometimes."

Coulda and Shoulda had leaned in so far, they fell in a heap next to Finn. Woulda ran for the fence, as the mice, still in their astronaut gear, chased him with their pirate cutlasses (left over from their performance in Sawyer's garage).

Alley Cat paid no attention to the other Realists and paced in front of Finn.

"Freedom, Huckleberry, is tricky," Alley Cat began. "An 'absence of undue restrictions,' as Collins English Dictionary defines it? Yes, yes. That's one way to describe freedom. Meaning what? Just this: no individual or government can inhibit what you say or think or write or express—unless, say, a Big Un is on television or radio or writes for a newspaper or a magazine. Then there are rules. The truth of the matter is there are almost always rules when it comes to freedom."

Finn never watched television with the Boy; it took too much time away from snoozing or playing basketball—not to mention that it stole away the Boy's attention. Finn didn't read either (dogs don't know how), but he enjoyed being read to, whether it was from the Blue Books or Merriam—or Collins, Merriam's kissing cousin.

"Are things not free if they have rules?" Finn asked.

"Oh, they are free, they are," Alley Cat answered. "But some have a very high cost. For instance, Big Uns feel that they have to protect the ears of their Young Uns, so no cuss words. They have to keep their Young Uns pure 'fore they send 'em off to war."

"Really?" the Lab gasped. He couldn't imagine the Boy fighting in a war.

"I'm being facetious, Finn," Alley Cat said. "But the Big Uns do sometimes try to trample on their own freedoms. They take sides against each other. Political parties, they call them. You've probably seen their lawn signs."

Finn nodded. "I've peed on some of them."

"Well, sometimes one party will try to squash the civil rights— 'the rights of personal liberty'—that the other party championed just to prove a point or to show how powerful they are.

"Oddly enough," the Count continued, "these groups sometimes come together (briefly) when the Young Uns are sent to fight the terrorists, who are vehemently opposed to civil rights."

Finn felt his world expanding.

Alley Cat went on: "Playing with civil rights in our country disrupts freedom. Rules are okay, necessary even; we can't have everybody doing *anything* they want—like robbing or killing someone. But it's dangerous to mess with civil rights, especially since things in this country are often cyclical—the real country, I mean, not one of Turtle's inside-outside distinctions. Imagine if you weren't allowed to bark anymore because all the stray cats came into power. Then imagine if the inverse was true, and the cats were forbidden to meow. It becomes a game of 'can't'. You *can't* do *this* because... You *can't* possibly say *that* because... Sometimes it becomes a matter of you *can't* do this or that because you're a certain color or believe in a different religion than those making the rules. *Can't* is a powerful word."

"And can't means won't," Coulda said, lifting his eye patch.

"Can't never could do anything," Shoulda said, shaking his head.

"Can't means won't," Woulda repeated quietly, "and won't means jail."

The Count rolled his eyes (again). "That's not what I meant—and that last part, Woulda, didn't make much sense and only applies to you. And it wasn't jail—it was worse; it was a kill shelter. But you escaped, so no pulling a sad face. The Wold is your oyster. We're relatively free."

Coulda asked, "But can't still means won't, right?"

Shoulda snapped the Siamese's eye patch strap.

Finn was surprised to see that Coulda had both of his eyes, but he was too confused to ask about it: "You said no one can stop me from expressing myself."

"True, true," Alley Cat replied. "Unless you want to take off your clothes in public (or in your case, your collar) or yell 'fire' in a movie theater (or a kennel) or pass wind in a crowded room."

"Poof!" Coulda said.

"Bottom burp," Shoulda added, gasping for air.

RRRIPPP, went Woulda's heinie. The other Realists stared at him, as if to say, *now really!*

Woulda, who'd succeeded in trapping the costumed mice in a corner of the patio, waved his hand in front of his malodorous, fuzzy bottom, and the two cornered mice fainted in exaggerated flourishes. (They were quite gifted actors.) Coulda approached on tiptoes and sprinkled something glittery over their supposedly comatose bodies. "Earlier I glittered all the other mice that live in the garage next door," Coulda said by way of explanation. "There were so many! I'm glad I brought extra Faerie dust." Finn nodded even though he didn't understand and shifted his focus back to Alley Cat, who was still lecturing.

"Censorship (to the Big Uns) is but a minor bending of freedom done, for instance, to save Young Uns from material that could make them bring a gun to school. Dogs aren't censored so much as they are bound by certain Big Un rules, but generally you can bark what you want. Our country is surely great compared to countries where the citizenry are beaten or threatened or beheaded," the Count explained, holding his nose, for Woulda's flatulence smelled like cheese that had been kept under a bed, inside a dirty sweat sock, for a month or more. "Our country is also great because of the central concept that all Big Uns and dogs and cats are created equal—which sounds better on paper, by the way, than it actually works in real life. (I'm thinking about kill shelters and houses of Hurters or Yellers.) Equality is a misunderstood concept. The antelope has certain freedoms never grasped by the lion, but in the end, the lion will lunch with the antelope, and in that dining experience (during which the antelope is the main course *and* the honored guest), all things *are* equal: two animals, lunch. Equality is the concept of all creatures having the same *opportunities*, which in our society is both true (in theory) and a pile of horse hockey (in reality), but *true* freedom is something else altogether."

Coulda and Shoulda marched behind the pacing Alley Cat, Coulda banging a pine cone like a drum, Shoulda blowing into a stick like a fife. Woulda busied himself fashioning (from a piece of fishing line) what looked like tiny nooses for the trapped mice.

Finn tried to follow Alley Cat's speech. He really, truly did. As best Finn could understand it, freedom required rules. Turtle had implied as much in a backwards kind of way. But still—what *was* freedom?

Alley Cat cleared his throat and said, "Freedom—let me tell you what freedom *isn't*. True freedom isn't about addiction—to alcohol or catnip, say. It's certainly not about the right to be violent towards others, such as shooting up a school or drowning kittens. While you're free to endlessly dream about a cathouse, you're not giving any thought to whether or not the felines within have their freedom or not."

Woulda, Coulda, and Shoulda froze, then walked in a little circle, examining the sky and whistling an old Irish sea shanty.

Alley Cat rolled his eyes for what seemed to Finn to be the hundredth time. (He half-expected the Count's eyes to roll out of his head.) Alley Cat continued: "Those things will tie you down. Addiction is slavery. Can't be free if you're tied to a chemical substance or a demagogue (someone who uses "prejudices and false claims…to gain power"). Can't be free if you're obsessed with someone else period. And violence often leads to *death* or a kind of one for the families of the slain. But here's the nitty-gritty: you're technically free to do *anything*, but there are laws and consequences."

The condemned mice took the opportunity to embrace freedom themselves. Woulda was too busy fretting about the aforementioned consequences to notice when the costumed mice ran off, fishing line nooses still around their scrawny necks. The mice were covered in Coulda's sparkles, his Faerie dust, and they glittered in the sunlight.

"*Death* is freedom in a way," Alley Cat said. "The final freedom."

Shoulda and Coulda fell over, clutching their chests. Woulda watched his fellow Realists, then did the same, landing in—you guessed it.

PLOP!

Alley Cat did his best to ignore his companions and said, "But our concern is about freedom right here, right now. The thing is, if you listen to the Big Uns (yours or someone else's), you'll hear all about Jesus or Muhammad or Yahweh or maybe even Buddha or Vishnu or this political ideology or that. Or worse: they have an existential crisis and believe that life lacks all meaning and even identity is confusing. Some Big Uns are tied to these ideas and beliefs, and inflexibility leads to a loss of freedom in a way, caused by the individual though, not by society."

Finn remembered hearing these some of these words when the Boy was doing a report he didn't want to do. (He was close to tears and even Finn dunking the basketball in the laundry basket couldn't bring the Boy out of his funk, but eventually he acclimated to high school, much to Finn's relief.) For the record, according Merriam, an ideology is a "systematic body of concepts especially about human life or culture," and existentialism is a "philosophical movement…centering on…individual existence" in an unknowable world, where the individual "must assume ultimate responsibility for acts of free will without any certain knowledge of what is right or wrong or good or bad," which could lead to the dreaded existential crisis.

Phew! Now that that's out of the way…

Coulda and Woulda used Finn's basketball as a pillow and watched Woulda scrape the poo from his chest—again.

Alley Cat said, "True freedom is this: don't hold on to anything too tight yet embrace everything while you can. The Wold's my home, Huckleberry. No boundaries, no turf wars."

Alley Cat lowered his voice: "I grew out of all that Jets and Sharks stuff when I was but a wee kitten. My leather gang jacket isn't real, but the boys love playacting, just like the mice.

"The creamy Lab was right when he said, " 'Home is wherever your ears are, and wherever your ears are, well, that's home.' But you can't hold onto it any more than you can hold onto a pretty butterfly that lands on your nose. You can only just enjoy it while it lasts. There's a freedom in having no attachments.

"Of course," Alley Cat mewed, "holding on to the theory of not holding on to anything is holding on to something, so it's a true enigma, this freedom. A paradox even. A riddle for the ages."

Finn scratched an ear. His head was filled and his stomach was empty and his Smart Bump didn't feel so smart.

"Turtle said fingerprints make us unique," Finn put forth.

"It almost goes without saying that you're unique," Alley Cat said. "Fingerprints or paw prints have little to do with it. Your best pal, Sawyer, is very wise. He just about nailed it when he barked, 'You are whatever you are—you can't change it or lose it.' You can change *and* remain the same at the core. For example, you can hold on to something as tight as you can, but as soon as it's gone, you're still here, but you're different. Freedom is knowing that. (Doesn't make it hurt any less though.) However, deep down, you're still the same dog."

"So…" Finn began, but words escaped him. Ideas and images swam about his Smart Bump.

"Still confused?" Alley Cat asked. "It's all tied together. Everything is."

Alley Cat clapped his paws. "Boys!" Shoulda raised his arms to the sky. Coulda licked his paw, held it in the air to feel which way the wind was blowing, then jumped, landing on top of Shoulda's head. Woulda took a running start, tripped on the basketball (which rolled dangerously close to the pile of poop), and instead of jumping, scaled Shoulda and Coulda (scratching the latter's nose something terrible) until he stood on the top of Coulda's noggin. Woulda reached blindly above his head with his paw.

Nothing was there.

Shoulda belched from the strain of being on the bottom, and the burp smelled like lunch meat. Finn swore his stomach was going to start eating itself if he didn't fill it with food soon.

Woulda stood on his tippy-toes and stretched and took hold of a long cord Finn hadn't seen hanging from the sky before and pulled on it. The sky went dark again, and Woulda lost his footing, flapping his arms like a bird before falling backwards to the ground, right into…

SQUISH!

Coulda, dying to scratch his wounded nose, did so in a furious, violent manner, which in turn tickled Shoulda's head, as he maintained his position on the bottom. Shoulda belched again, loud and hard enough to knock Coulda off balance. The Siamese cat fell on top of some annoyed black mice who were just on their way to their next gig (at the behest of Alley Cat).

Woulda cleaned the poop off his toes and sniffed the belch-infested air.

"Bologna?"

Finn tried not to laugh, but the Realists were a funny lot—like watching puppies.

"*Ahem!*" Alley Cat cleared his throat and spit a hairball. The still-sparkly mice (and their glittery friends and relatives from the garage) hugged each other and ran up the dogwood or the sycamore. They were all dressed as astronauts for the upcoming performance. Each had a piece of fishing line tied around their little waists.

"If you will turn your attention once again to the sky…" Alley Cat instructed, and when Finn did, he forgot all about his Little White Tie and empty belly, his orange-and-blue-striped basketball and Woulda cleaning off excrement yet again.

The sky was crowded with what seemed like a thousand blinking diamonds, more precious than any stuffed animal or tennis ball Finn had ever owned.

"Stars," Alley Cat said.

Shoulda lay on his back and stretched himself on the ground, and Coulda leaned his noggin on his companion's stomach. A few feet away, Woulda lay in the grass and crossed his arms behind his fuzzy head. Finn heard the sound of giggling mice coming from the sky.

"You've heard the expression: a blanket of stars?" Alley Cat asked. Finn hadn't, but it sounded nice, better than the Blanket of the Lordy. The stars twinkled and winked at him.

"They're as unique as fingerprints because each one has its own spectrum, which is similar to the spectrum of colors you see in a rainbow. Identification is what fingerprints and the like are all about. Every Big Un generally has more than one fingerprint, but each is unique. Every animal has paw prints or something along the same lines. I don't know what snakes have, but maybe their trails make them unique. Admittedly, I've only known one garter snake, but I could always tell when he was around. Paw prints, fingerprints: those are how we identify each other sight unseen—one way anyhow. (Animals rely more on smell.) We need to recognize one another, especially if we're lost like you are. We need to be able to tell friends from enemies. We need clues. The stars—they don't need anything. They're just stars, and that's enough. The spectra are just how scientists identify them. In fact, Huckleberry, the way I understand it is that most of the stars are already *d*ead."

Finn gasped and jumped back, sitting on Woulda accidentally, who released a smidgen of gas.

"No, no. Don't worry," Alley Cat said. "They're not going anywhere. (The real ones anyway.) I don't know why or how, but every night, the stars, *d*ead or not, are always up there. A blanket of stars? Sure, but this blanket doesn't cover your eyes from the rest of the Wold like Turtle's armor does, nor does it require the rest of the Wold to climb under there with you like Pig's Blanket of the Lordy. Stars don't think they're better than you just 'cause they're up in the sky and burn real bright, so bright that we can still see 'em long after they're *d*ead. Stars are concerned with being stars, not tied to any one school of thought or Goodly Book. A bit altruistic actually, the stars, being *d*ead and all but still leaving their light for us to enjoy, while it's hard to pry an almost empty can of tuna from a dead cat's paws."

Woulda crawled out from under Finn's behind. Shoulda and Coulda sat next to the Lab on either side, rubbing against him.

"And Huckleberry?" Alley Cat said. "If there is a God, a Lordy, an Is, then surely among the first things created were the stars, for much of what the first creatures needed to learn were in the skies, namely life and *d*eath, although they didn't know it yet."

Finn stared at the stars with Count Bjørn de Vagabond and the Realists. Even Woulda stopped cleaning himself to smile at the sky. Finn stared and stared, following one shooting star after another with his eyes until his lids grew heavy, and when he opened them, Alley Cat was sitting in front of him, nose to nose, but the sky was back to its late afternoon grey. Shoulda and Coulda had crept away and snoozed beneath the dogwood tree, nestled among its fallen leaves. Coulda's eye patch had slipped down to his nose. (He only wore it for aesthetic purposes anyway.) Woulda rolled in the grass (and into a puddle) in a final attempt to wash up before joining his fellow Realists for a nap. The glittery black mice and their relations and friends had lowered themselves to the ground and were untangling the fishing lines that dangled from the branches of the dogwood and the sycamore. They brushed the Faerie dust from each other's shoulders, removed their astronaut costumes, and took a bologna break before going back into hiding. (Fun and games aside, there were cats around, though the Realists never hurt any of them. However they did chase the mice now and again—and make nooses.)

"Understand?" Alley Cat asked, and Finn nodded his head. But there was one thing…

"Are my ears made of *SILK*?" Finn asked quietly. "The Boy told me they were a thousand times. And I want to know: what is *SILK* and are my ears made of it?"

"Your one big question has become two," Alley Cat said. "Don't worry about what *SILK* is. It's enough to know that it's as wondrous as you are, and you are wondrous, inside and out—for a dog," he said with a smile.

Alley Cat kissed Finn on his big, black nose.

"You, my friend, have the gift of Absolute Love," Alley Cat said. "Not many of us get that gift, but it comes at a great cost. For anything we love can be gone in an instant. (I wish I could be as open as you with love.) To know your true nature and embrace it: that is a kind of freedom, and I envy you for it just a little, Huckleberry, and I pray for you too, for the worst pain of all is the pain of not being loved back. Nothing else even comes close."

Finn started to cry, and when he looked up, Alley Cat was crying too.

"Come here, my friend," the Count said, leading him towards the largest puddle in the backyard, the one that Finn thought looked familiar.

At the edge of the puddle, Alley Cat put both paws on Finn's noggin.

"What I'm going to show you, Huckleberry, is the Most Absolute Truth of All."

"The Most Absolute Truth," Finn repeated.

Alley Cat stepped back and sat next to Finn.

The puddle shimmered; a slight breeze tickled the water and made it laugh. Alley Cat leaned over so his face looked straight down into the puddle. Finn could hear the Realists snoring gently beneath the dogwood tree (except for Woulda, who sounded like an asthmatic tuba).

The puddle settled down, current by current, until the late afternoon sky stared back at Finn and Alley Cat.

"Your answer is there," the Count said, gesturing with his nose at the puddle, and Finn peered in.

Finn had seen his reflection in a puddle before, but he usually splashed around too much if he was playing or was very thirsty. But it was different this time. Finn had never given his reflection much attention (other than in the garage when he was on the bouncy circle, though he was moving too fast to be contemplative), but something caught his eye in the puddle and refused to let go.

"Ask your question," Alley Cat said.

Finn leaned his muzzle as close to the water as he could; his runny, black nose was an inch away from the surface.

"Are my ears made of *SILK*?" Finn asked.

His breath stirred the water and everything went blurry. Finn's Little White Tie just about stopped.

"It's going away, Count," Finn cried. "It's leaving."

"Ask again," Alley Cat said.

"Are my ears made of *SILK*?" Finn breathed into the puddle. Again, the surface of the puddle shimmered and drifted. The reflected sky lost its shape and returned.

"Once more," Alley Cat said, and he stepped back lest he contribute to the shimmering of the puddle and watched as the black Lab asked a third time.

Finn held his breath, and the water fell still, and there, in the middle of the shiny puddle, were the most beautiful, the softest-looking, the most...well...*SILKIEST* things he'd ever seen. When Finn tilted his noggin, the *SILK* rose and dipped lazily. When Finn expressed surprise, the *SILK* rose up a slight bit, as if listening intently to a far off sound. And when Finn turned his noggin back and forth? Two pieces of *SILK* flapped in the puddle!

Alley Cat's reflection appeared over Finn's shoulder.

"They're my ears?" Finn barked. "Count Bjørn, Count Bjørn— my ears *are* made of *SILK*!"

"Of course they are," Alley Cat said, sheathing his claws to pet Finn's ears. "You almost always know the answers. You were just asking the wrong creatures, meaning the Vicar Pig and Colonel Turtle. When Sawyer showed you what I just did (in his own way with the bouncy circle and the mirror), you just weren't ready to believe because you thought you were in a dream."

"All this is *real*?" asked Finn, and the Count answered yes. The Lab took a few minutes to take it all in: his Great Journey, his quest.

"I feel..." Finn began. "I'm not sure *better* is the right word, but *different*. A good *D* word: different. And different is sometimes better, right?"

"You would know," Alley Cat said.

The other Realists woke up and took turns petting Finn's *SILK*.

"Look one more time," Alley Cat said, "before the sun starts to descend any further," and Finn leaned over to peer into the puddle again. "See the grey snout? See the long silvery eyebrows sprouting out? Change, Huckleberry. Change. Your skin gets tougher and looser, you run a little slower. Look at me. I'm all tufts. But tufts equal toughness."

Storm clouds rolled in and soon it was just another muddy puddle, but Finn had seen what the Count had pointed out.

Alley Cat knocked on Finn's noggin.

"Same for the brain," Count Bjørn said. "Grows tougher, more stuck in its ways, maybe a wee bit slower too, but this," Alley Cat said, touching his paw to Little White Tie, "this never stays tough long."

Alley Cat lowered his mews to a whisper.

"You will learn to love again, my friend. The gang doesn't want to hear it sometimes. Ruins their image as street warriors."

Shoulda and Coulda had grown bored of petting Finn and had turned on Woulda, petting Woulda's ears with his own tail, a display of affection not entirely appreciated by the grey bundle of Woulda.

"Learn to love again," Alley Cat whispered. "That's the trick. That's the answer to both of your other questions too. Freedom? Just knowing you'll love again, that's freedom enough. Dying? Who knows? So love what you can while you can.

"Your ears, Huckleberry, aren't the only things you have made of *SILK*," Alley Cat said. "They're just the beginning."

Thunder rolled in the heavens, and Finn shivered. (Baron Thunder—Mr. Boom—was an unwelcome guest.) Shoulda and Coulda, who'd lifted Woulda off the ground for a game of catch, dropped him, accidentally—in you know what!

Alley Cat snapped his finger-knives to attention.

"The time has come for you to go home, Huckleberry Finn," Alley Cat said.

Finn looked up, his eyes and nostrils wide.

"Where is my home now?"

"You're adopted," Alley Cat said. "Home is wherever you lay your head—while you still have it."

Woulda, Coulda, and Shoulda surrounded Finn. Alley Cat flashed his finger knives, and the dying sun glinted from their sharp ends to Finn's eyes.

"I thought I was going to be a Realist," Finn said, looking from one cat to another. "Aren't I one of you?"

Alley Cat raised his claws in the air and the Realists did the same. *SWOOP!*

In one swift arc, the finger-knives came down and sliced the surface of the puddle. Finn watched his reflection wave goodbye. Finn lifted his paw too.

"You are in your own Kingdom, your own backyard," Alley Cat said. "Do you not recognize it?"

And Finn did, from the tall wooden fence to the dogwood and sycamore trees to the old mimosa stump and the hole in the fence behind the shed. He even recognized the white garage in Sawyer's Kingdom. In fact, he could hear Sawyer and Becky barking to one another. Echo and some of the other rabbits peeked out from under the shed. Jenny and Agnes sang from the dogwood, soon to go wherever birds go during a storm. The Realists kept turning Finn in a circle so he could take it all in.

"You are family, Huckleberry," Alley Cat said. "You always were."

Woulda, Coulda, and Shoulda embraced Finn in a massive hug, promising to visit soon, writing down his jacket size, and showing him, as quick as possible, the secret Realist handshake. Woulda made sure to wipe away the little bit of poo he'd rubbed on Finn's fur, but Finn figured it was his own poop that Woulda was seemingly magnetically attracted to, so he smiled and barked hardy farewells. Even the original pair of black mice came out of hiding to pat Finn's paw. One was dressed as a pirate, the other an astronaut. Both were still a little glittery. Finn heaped compliments on their performances.

There exploded in the sky more thunder (the mice headed for the hills)—followed by the siren call of an intruder. Another dog? A Big Un? Turtle with his army or Pig with his congregation?

The Realists—save Alley Cat—disappeared over the wooden fence.

Then Alley Cat and Finn hugged goodbye in the din of the coming storm, and this hug became legendary. And although its importance in relations between dogs and cats can never be understated, the Legend of the Hug grew to such extremes that little kittens wrote careful letters in cursive to Finn and Bjørn, who never failed (with the help of the kittens' parental units) to deliver a present to each and every one of them on the anniversary of the embrace.

Puppies were taught the hug as the symbolic beginning of a treaty between cats and dogs, a treaty so long in coming that (according to the Legend) the heavens had rained down dog cookies and cat treats upon its undertaking. So every year on the date of the hug, puppies and their parents sit down to share an extra cookie or two and give thanks and praise to two so wise, Bjørn and Finn, that the Lordy or Good God Almighty or the Is, had seen fit to rain down treats for all. And then all the dogs would hug and promise, at least for that day, not to chase cats, even if they climbed into their Kingdoms or danced on the fence tops.

And rain down it did on that very special day (but not cookies, not really), drenching both Alley Cat and Finn.

"I'm going to miss you, Count," Finn cried softly.

Footsteps on the patio. Shouts. A door slamming shut.

"I'll miss you too," Alley Cat said. "Maybe you can chase me around the backyard tomorrow if the weather breaks."

Finn ran in a circle around his friend.

"If I find a home, do you want me to see if you can move in too?" Finn asked, his tail wagging, Little White Tie thumping.

THUMP THUMP THUMP *BUMP!*

THUMP THUMP THUMP *BUMP!*

Alley Cat smiled and spread his arms as if to embrace the backyard.

"I'm already home," Alley Cat said. "Everywhere is my home."

Finn smiled back and let his long tongue hang out.

"You've taught me so much, Count. I'm so glad I'm in the gang and that you're the leader and—"

The footsteps were near the edge of the patio. They'd reach the grass any second now.

"Believe in yourself, Huckleberry," Alley Cat urged. "Don't believe in me. Besides: everything I said could be wrong."

And that was what Alley Cat said.

Count Bjørn climbed the wooden fence as the sky really opened up and it began to pour. He raised his paw (Finn did the same) and jumped out of this book (for now) and into the wide Wold.

The footsteps reached the grass. The Lab thought he was a Goner.

"Finn!" the Boy cried, splashing through the mud towards the black Lab.

"Finn!" Mommy Big Un cried, not minding that the Lab was muddy, not one bit. "Where were you? We really have to fix that hole in the fence."

"Get out of the rain, old man," Daddy Big Un said, quite cheerfully.

When the Boy hugged Finn so long that both of them became soaked to their bones, it became the second most written about and discussed hug in history, just after the one between Finn and the Count. For the Boy loved Finn and thought of Finn as a brother. Growing up was hard work and required more time and effort than being a Boy did. Finn would learn to understand this in time: the Boy was growing older, but Finn wasn't. Oh sure, maybe in actual years (dog years or Big Un years, it doesn't matter), but Finn, like all dogs, remained a puppy inside. He just moved at a slower pace and napped more than usual.

The Boy knelt in the mud and caressed Finn's ears.

"*SILK*," the Boy said.

Finn's Little White Tie almost broke free of its cage. The Great Journey had been long and hard on Finn's "heart," but Little White Ties have ways of beating through even the worst storms.

Learn to love again, Alley Cat had whispered in Finn's *SILK* ears, but the retriever had never really forgotten how.

"Come home, Finn," the Boy said, and Finn bounded after him, shaking away the rain before he stepped through the sliding glass door (careful not to wake the turtle). He went through the family room (ignoring the squeak of the guinea pig), up the stairs (where Mommy Big Un bathed him and rubbed him dry with a soft towel), and eventually into the Boy's room. There he jumped into bed and waited for the Boy to finish brushing and flossing, so Finn could tell him everything he'd learned and so the Boy could rub his ears and belly and read to him from the Blue Books, and whisper...

Finn fell asleep.

+

A Few Minutes Later:

The orange-and-blue-striped basketball rolled in the wind of the rainstorm and landed in the puddle where Finn had seen his reflection. The backyard was deserted. Alley Cat climbed back over the fence and, with much difficulty, stuffed the basketball into his imaginary pocket and became one with the night.

Episode VII

What Becomes *SILK*

Finn wasn't quite the Goner he'd thought. Mommy Big Un said he'd caught cold from staying outside in the rain. Finn's bones were weary, his nose runny, and his stomach rumbly. After a quick dinner and a couple of cookies, Finn was bundled into a blanket on the Boy's bed, and when the Big Uns closed the door, the Boy woke the Lab to hug him tight and read to him.

The books the Boy read to Finn that night (and many other nights after) weren't Blue Books. Finn didn't mind at all, but as both the Boy and Finn grew older, Finn noticed the Blue Books were growing beards of fine, grey dust. And in the middle of the front cover of *The Missing Chums*: a tiny fingerprint, surely too tiny for the Boy who looked bigger to Finn every day. And the smudge next to the little fingerprint? Why, that was Finn's nose print! He'd have recognized his nose print anywhere! It was as unique as a star.

One rainy afternoon, while the Boy was in school, Mommy Big Un charged into the room with what looked like a fluffy bird on a stick and attacked the Blue Books. Dust flew everywhere! Then she placed the books in a big cardboard box. Mommy Big Un was quite determined. Finn stuck his nose in the box and cried a little. He knew the Blue Books were leaving.

"He's too old for the Hardy Boys, Finn," Mommy Big Un said.

She lugged the box into the attic, and Finn never saw the Blue Books again...except the one that the Boy had placed with the volumes that had been deemed "age appropriate" by the Big Uns. It was in a place of honor on the shelf above the Boy's bed.

Finn's days were spent much as they had been before his Great Journey. During the week, he'd help the Boy get ready for school. (Unless it was snowing; on those days, the Boy and Finn huddled beneath the blankets, feeling very much a team, waiting to hear the Boy's school number announced on the radio; if it was, Finn knew, the day could be spent building snow forts, throwing snowballs, and eating snow; Finn liked to eat snow.) Then Finn would spend the hours after lunch napping, moving from room to room to avoid Mommy Big Un and the monster Vacuum. At night, the Boy and Finn would horse around with the Lab's much cherished stuffed animals or play fetch with Finn's new green-and-black-striped basketball (for, despite his best efforts, he'd lost his prize orange-and-blue-striped basketball during his Great Journey). But the Boy had lots and lots of homework, and sometimes other loud boys came over to listen to music, and every once in a while, a girl would stop by and the Boy would blush.

Finn still went into his backyard Kingdom to go to the bathroom, and when it was nice, he'd cruise the fence line, looking for Count Bjørn and the Realists, but they were gone, and no amount of hoping, it seemed, would bring them back. He still had Sawyer and Becky and Jim, and the creamy Lab took them on many swell adventures, pirates being a big problem in their neck of the woods.

Then there came the day when the Vicar Pig caught cold. He didn't last long—guinea pigs rarely do once they catch cold. Mommy Big Un gave Pig colored liquid in an eyedropper, but the Vicar *d*ied anyway. Shortly before he did, Finn visited him in the family room.

"Mr. Vicar," Finn whispered (or tried to), "are you awake?"

Pig lifted his head from his blanket of torn-up newspapers.

"Is that you, O Lordy?" Pig asked. "Or are you an angel?"

"No," Finn said. "I'm a Lab. It's Finn. Remember me?"

"Finish who? Why are you taking me, O Lordy? I've been your faithful servant. I've spread your word. I've condemned your enemies and made new ones for you. I've—"

"Would you like me to move that piece of carrot or the slice of celery closer?" Finn interrupted.

"The only thing I need is the Goodly Book," Pig said.

"I don't have one of those," Finn replied.

"Gosh darn dog…" Pig said, and then he was gone.

Finn was sad for his passing and watched as Daddy Big Un dug Pig a little hole in the backyard.

The Colonel Turtle would soon be in a hole next to the Vicar Pig—a positioning that neither party would have much appreciated. The Colonel was old when he *d*ied. When the Boy first said Turtle was ill, Finn went to visit the Colonel at his aquarium near the sliding glass door that led to the country the reptile called Pat-ti-o., but Turtle wouldn't come out of his shell, which looked worn from age and battles past.

"How could they do this?" Turtle's shell asked.

"Who?" Finn asked back. "What did they do?"

"*They*, soldier!" Turtle's shell thundered. "We tried to stop them. In my day, we'd have crushed them like we did the pinkos. Now—why, just look at the news! *They're* everywhere! Do the math! Look at the clues! Conjugate the verbs! We need a sneak attack. We need Special Ops. We need Black Ops. We need—"

Finn left. He never could figure out who *they* were. And soon enough, the war was over for the Colonel. Turtle was buried next to Pig in a ceremony attended only by Finn and Daddy Big Un. The Boy didn't like these kinds of ceremonies, Daddy Big Un said, and Finn understood. Finn didn't like these kinds of ceremonies either.

Then one day: what he never thought would happen again happened.

One short whistle. One long. Another short.

Finn had been cruising the fence line, enjoying the sunshine and the cool breeze. He'd paid his respects to Pig and Turtle, as he did every time he went out to what the Colonel had called the Fields of Backyard. Now he was just sauntering, barking at Mr. Nutball Jr. (Mr. Nutball Sr. had met his end during an encounter with Mr. Beckett's Cadillac) or listening to Jenny and Agnes and the other birds, while chasing dandelion wishes.

Again: one short whistle—one long—another short.

Finn stepped away from the fence, and there he was: a little ragged, a trifle skinny, but it was him, and Finn's Little White Tie pounded double time, then triple time.

"Count Bjørn!" Finn barked.

"It is I," Alley Cat said, spinning on his toes.

"And the Realists?" Finn asked, turning his head back and forth, his tongue hanging out.

There was a rustle on the other side of the fence, then Coulda appeared, looking *really* skinny, but still quite regal in his Siamese coat and eye patch, followed by Shoulda, still chunky, but missing patches of fur here and there. They all looked cool in their imaginary leather jackets.

"The Realists!" Finn cried, and the cats leapt from the fence, and they all danced and exchanged paw shakes.

"I thought you'd forgotten all about me," Finn said.

"Not at all, my brother," Alley Cat replied. "But Woulda…"

Coulda and Shoulda bowed their heads.

"He's… Woulda's the *D* word?" Finn asked.

"No," Coulda said, choking back tears.

"Adopted," Alley Cat explained.

"But wait," Finn said. "I'm adopted!" he reminded them.

And once the Realists digested this bit of realism, they hugged and danced once more, and they broke out the vittles and the vino and raised their imaginary glasses to Woulda.

"May he crack nuts," Alley Cat said, "forever!"

Coulda and Shoulda shouted the customary response: "May he forever break the wind! May he forever cut the cheese!" And Finn joined in on the refrain of "Forever! Forever!"

The Realists then gave Finn his imaginary leather gang jacket. (They'd been carrying it around for a long time, but the wear and tear gave it an appropriate toughness.) It didn't fit—cats were smaller than Labrador retrievers, but Shoulda draped it from the top of Finn's noggin, and even though it wasn't really there, all four of them saw it, and the strays admired the way Finn looked in it.

"So, that's where we've been. We tried to break him out a dozen times," Coulda said.

"I think he likes it there," Alley Cat admitted. "Strays who are adopted learn to like living in houses."

Finn agreed, and as they lay in the grass, he filled the Realists in on everything that had happened since they'd last met.

When Finn was done, Alley Cat winked at Coulda and Shoulda.

"Are you ready?" Alley Cat asked Finn.

Finn jumped up and wagged his tail.

"You bet I am!"

"Okay, rules are: there are no rules," Alley Cat said. "Just nothing too real, okay?"

"Okay!" Coulda, Shoulda, and Finn shouted.

And so the Games began.

The Games took place every day at roughly noon (with the offspring of the costumed mice acting as referees, cheerleaders, and, occasionally, quarry). Sawyer, who had an overactive imagination, frequently joined in and was made a member of the Realists too. Once in a while, they played at night, and sometimes they tried mornings, but the Big Uns always yelled at the noise. (Woulda joined them as often as he could escape, but he was quite comfortable in his new home, thank you very much.) When Shoulda *died* (he choked on a bologna sandwich that wasn't his, an unfortunate turn of events, but Shoulda liked his bologna), the remaining Realists held a Memorial Game in his honor. When Coulda passed away at an old age, Finn, Sawyer, and Alley Cat donned imaginary eye patches and dedicated a Game to their fallen comrade. Becky joined in and after he broke out (again) so did Jim. Coulda, it turned out, had been a collector—of fallen stars. His pockets were full of them (the fact that they were imaginary—the pockets *and* the stars—meant little), and they were covered with Faerie dust. In addition, there were a couple of stunned mice in there. His friends watched over him during his last moments, and even as his breath took leave of his golden Siamese body, the stars in his pockets winked and shined. He'd strung them together with fishing wire to form a necklace, and they glittered and sputtered and looked nothing at all like Finn thought they would.

"The big picture, Huckleberry," Alley Cat said, "rarely looks anything like you think it will.

"But in the end," the Count added, "everything is connected."

Woulda managed to sneak out for both burials, which took place in Finn's Kingdom, for his Big Uns were sympathetic to strays. (Woulda had been so overcome with grief at Shoulda's funeral, he insisted that his portly pal be buried with what remained of the deadly bologna sandwich.) But by the time of Coulda's interment, Woulda's flatulence had reached such extreme proportions that he was forced to attend the service from behind the high wooden fence.

Alley Cat bowed his head and read from one of the Hardy Boys' Blue Books—*The Missing Chums* to be exact (which Finn had fetched from the Boy's shelf), for it was truly a Goodly Book. This was the passage Alley Cat read:

"Frank! Joe!" cried Chet, overjoyed. As soon as his hands were untied, the stout boy grabbed his pals and hugged them in excitement.

"Amen," said the chorus of astronaut and pirate mice offspring.

"Amen," said Finn.

Nothing more needed to be said.

Woulda broke wind on the other side of the fence.

RRRIPPP!

"How does he look?" Woulda yelled.

"He looks *d*ead," Alley Cat shouted back.

RRRIPPP!

"Sorry," Woulda said. "Excuse me."

"You don't want to see him," Alley Cat yelled. "It's better if you don't."

"Okay," Woulda yelled back. "Is he shining? The stars in his pockets—are they shining?"

"Always," Alley Cat said, as the last of the dirt was shoveled over his old pal's body.

"So much for our brand of Realism," Alley Cat whispered to Finn and Sawyer.

"What?" Woulda shouted.

"Nothing," Alley Cat said.

RRRIPPP!

"Sorry," Woulda said. "Excuse me—again."

When Woulda *d*ied, he died farting. At least that was the word on the streets of the Wold. Woulda's adopted parents had tried to hide Woulda's *d*emise from their Girl, but when the Girl found her parents burying Woulda, wrapped in an old Star Wars blanket, in a hastily dug hole, she squeezed the mangy, old cat so hard, he released his last bit of gas.

SQUEAK!

Legend in the neighborhood had it that you could still smell Woulda's final escaped wind on the anniversary of his *d*eath. And, the legend continued, in deference to his old partner, Shoulda, it smelled very much like bologna.

Finn and Alley Cat and Sawyer met just about every morning and afternoon to relive the past. They tried to continue the Games, but even the black mice's offspring had passed away, and *their* offspring (and successive generations) had little time for costumes or three old Realists. (Sawyer had finally gotten his imaginary gang jacket and wore it every day, even when it was hot outside).

One afternoon, shortly before Finn caught an illness he wasn't able to shake (his legs ached, his breathing grew labored, and a lump developed on his side), he and Alley Cat lounged in a sunspot in the Lab's backyard Kingdom.

"It's been an extraordinarily Great Journey," Finn said, watching a dandelion wish fall like a star.

Alley Cat yawned and snuggled closer to Finn.

"It's not quite over yet," the Count said.

"I know," Finn replied.

And he did know—in the way that dogs know their owners are sad or angry or happy. Finn wanted to see the Boy graduate from high school. But inside his Little White Tie, Finn knew his attendance wasn't a reality.

"Will I see you again, once—?" Finn couldn't finish.

"I love you," Alley Cat said. He didn't know the answer.

"I love you," Finn said.

"You saved me," Finn added.

"You saved you," Alley Cat mewed. "And then you saved me."

"It's a mystery," Finn concluded.

"No, not really," Alley Cat said after a long pause. "We all learned to love again. The only mystery is why we lost love in the first place."

Sawyer, Becky, and Jim soon joined them and then, briefly, the Boy. The Lab felt complete and napped the day away.

In general, inside and outside the house, Finn slept even more than before. He tended his morning duties, made sure the Boy got off to school okay, ate a cookie with Mommy Big Un, and then would spend the rest of the day sleeping. He went outside only when he had to use the bathroom or share a secret with Alley Cat or plan a small adventure with Sawyer. (Planning was all they could do at their age.) Mommy Big Un didn't want Finn sleeping in the yard. She gave him medicine that tasted like rancid cherries, Daddy Big Un rubbed the inside of Finn's old ears with ointment, and a grey-haired, kind doctor tended to Finn's lump.

And the Boy: the Boy grew into a young man, and Finn's Little White Tie beat a frantic tempo whenever he caught sight of the Boy in the act of growing up: dressing up in a funny suit for something called a prom, getting grounded for sharing a beer with a buddy behind the shed (Alley Cat filled Finn in on the details), kissing a girl named Mary Lou (who smelled like vanilla milkshakes!) over and over again on the old sofa in the basement.

Finn knew he would leave the Boy soon, and he had to swallow a different kind of lump whenever he thought of this. Finn didn't know where he was going; Alley Cat and Sawyer didn't know either. But Finn knew this: it would be a Great Journey of a Different Sort. Finn was ready for whatever was next, but he was scared just the same, for he so loved the Boy and the Big Uns and Alley Cat and Sawyer and the retrievers. Not seeing them anymore—there was nothing scarier to Finn. Not even thunderstorms or fireworks.

When the day came—it was a beautiful fall day—Finn lay in the Boy's bed trying to find his breath. He'd climbed into bed with it, but it was running away from him. Finn wanted to chase after his breath and retrieve it. He was good at retrieving. But Finn knew, inside his Little White Tie, that *this* was his Last Great Journey in the Wold.

The Boy was crying, and Finn licked his face.

Daddy and Mommy Big Un were crying too, but Finn couldn't reach them with his tongue. They rubbed his belly, which went up and down, up and down, up and down, as if trying to make up for Little White Tie. Finn's Little White Tie was coming undone.

"Good dog," Daddy Big Un said.

"Do you want a cookie, Finn?" Mommy Big Un asked, but this one time, he didn't.

Maybe he'd see Woulda, Coulda, and Shoulda where he was going.

Maybe he'd see his mom.

Outside, a cat howled into the falling of the leaves, and a dog yelped back.

The Boy leaned his face against Finn's. Finn wagged his tail and managed a little growl that said, "I love you." Finn hoped the Boy understood. (He did.)

The Boy lowered his mouth against Finn's ear and whispered.

The Boy whispered in his ear.

"A Lab's ears are made of *SILK*," the Boy whispered, and Finn knew it was true.

Little White Tie beat once, twice, three times...

+

A Few Minutes Later:

Finn was buried in the backyard, beneath the dogwood tree. The Boy and Daddy Big Un had wrapped Finn in the Boy's blanket and had laid Finn's stuffed animals—Monkey and Frog and Elephant and Panda—next to him, along with the old copy of *The Missing Chums*, the greatest of all the Hardy Boy's mystery adventures. Sawyer dropped in his best tennis ball, while Becky and Jim offered up their favorite toys. Lastly, the Boy added the green-and-black-striped basketball. When Daddy Big Un shoveled the first load of dirt upon the blanket and Monkey and Frog and Elephant and Panda and the gifts from the retrievers, as well as the well-read copy of *The Missing Chums* and the newer basketball, the Boy sobbed so loud, Finn could hear him from where he'd been watching, high above the clouds, nestled in between the stars. Woulda, Coulda, and Shoulda were there, as well as lots of mice in costumes. Finn's mom was waiting for him. (She was more beautiful than Finn had remembered.) They were all stars, and when they fell, as stars do, they were only playing a game, dipping their light into the great big wide Wold below.

Once Finn learned how, he fell every night to whisper (really whisper) into the Boy's ear, and he rose again to shine light upon the Great Journeys the Boy had yet to take but one day would. Wherever the Boy went, a star of absolute *SILK* made his way a little brighter, for the paths would sometimes be thorny and dark, and Finn wanted the Boy to know they were all *SILK* and *SILK* they would all remain.

+

Too:

The last of the original Realists waited on top of the fence until the Big Uns and the Boy had gone inside. The Boy went in last, after sitting for a long time beside the mound of earth that marked the beginning of Finn's Last Great Journey. The Boy never stopped crying, and when he finally went in (it was growing dark and more than a little chilly), Alley Cat hopped down and realized that what he had taken for rain were his own tears, and the dogs took turns hugging him (and each other).

Sawyer was the next to go, and Alley Cat oversaw that ceremony too. Sawyer's Big Uns tried to shoo him away—what was an old cat doing at a dog's funeral?—but they knew nothing of the Legend of the Hug. The Count made sure Sawyer was buried with a boatload of dandelions. Maybe one of them would smell different.

Alley Cat was old and felt every passing year. His fur was matted, and his eyesight wasn't what it used to be. The stars, on certain nights, threw enough light for him to get around. Alley Cat hurt everywhere; even his toes were in pain. He knew his own Last Great Journey would start soon. He was ready. He missed his friends. He missed the Games and Sawyer's adventures. He even missed Woulda's flatulence, although Alley Cat farted enough these last, long days for the whole gang. He thought of it as gas to help him take off for the stars—and he hoped the stars called soon, so he could stop hurting and be with his friends.

Alley Cat sat next to the mound of earth marking Finn's grave on the anniversary of the Lab's passing. He rolled in the dirt, rubbed his face in it, tried to snuggle next to it. It was no use; he still missed his friend fiercely.

When he rose from the dirt, Alley Cat was every inch the regal Count Bjørn de Vagabond of legend, and he reached into the pocket of his imaginary leather jacket.

His paws shook, but he never dropped the ball, which, until this very moment, he'd forgotten he had.

"*SILK*," the Count said.

Alley Cat kissed the orange-and-blue-striped basketball and placed it on top of the mound of dirt.

"We are all *SILK*," Alley Cat said before falling asleep next to the basketball.

And that night and all his remaining nights, Alley Cat dreamed of the stars.

And when, soon after, the stars called him by his full name, Alley Cat ascended slowly, for he'd remembered to bring Finn's basketball at the last second.

Oh, the games we'll play, Alley Cat thought, and then Alley Cat was a Goner too.

-end-

Thank you:

Kathleen Rose Harrington
Kathleen Rose Cronk

My First Reader and cover artist Nichole Kohler
Cooper Miller, my co-First Reader

Beth Meier, who worked on the original version included in
Saving Magdalene and took care of the formatting for this one

Pepper Lillie's Steve Brandsdorfer & Dominique Messihi,
who designed the cover

Kimberly Hitchens of Booknook.biz

Justin Wallace
Mitch Rothschild
Wayne Aretz

Mighty Mike Berson
Craig Do'Vidio
Stephanie Hollister

About the Author

Michael-Patrick has been the proud Pops of two of the greatest Labrador retrievers ever to be born: Raven (Helium Raven Teardrop) and Duke (Sir Duke).

The author adopted Raven in 2003. The black Lab was almost six. He loved playing basketball. He passed away the day after his fourteenth birthday.

Duke was adopted when he was five in 2020. Duke is a yellow Lab, but he came out cream-colored except for three yellow spots.

Adopting Raven and Duke were the best decisions the author ever made. Finn and Sawyer are Michael-Patrick's tributes to his boys.

Michael-Patrick supports the following charity organizations:

o   National Multiple Sclerosis Society: nationalmssociety.org

o   Brookline Labrador Retriever Rescue: brooklinelabrescue.org

o   RAINN (Rape, Abuse, & Incest National Network): RAINN.org

o   National Education Alliance for Borderline Personality Disorder: borderlinepersonalitydisorder.com

o   Borderline Personality Disorder Resource Center: nyp.org/bpdresourcecenter